Chris is a newcomer to Green Hill. His family has settled in, even his brother, who made the mistake of trying to take the alpha position from the Green Hill pride alpha, but not Chris. He feels like he doesn't belong, and he doesn't know how to fix it.

Meeting his mate might help.

Drake is in love with love, but love doesn't work for him. Every time he's in a relationship, he gets dumped because of his personality — he's too needy, he talks too much or expects too much from his boyfriend. He hasn't given up, but when he meets his mate, he decides that something needs to change before he sends Chris running, too.

That something is him.

While Chris does his best to get to know the real Drake, Drake does his best to hide his personality from Chris. The push and pull is maddening for both of them and can't continue forever, but who will win?

Christopher
Copyright © 2024 Catherine Lievens
ISBN: 978-1-4874-4235-4
Cover art by Angela Waters

Published by eXtasy Books Inc

Look for us online at:
www.eXtasybooks.com

CHRISTOPHER
GREEN HILL PRIDE 11

BY

CATHERINE LIEVENS

CHAPTER ONE

Chris felt out of place, but then how could he feel at home when he was surrounded by a bunch of tigers?

Part of him felt like he wasn't supposed to be here. He was supposed to be back home with the pack, in the place where he'd been born. He would still be there if his family hadn't had to move.

All because their alpha had kicked his brother out.

Chris scowled at the wall, since he couldn't scowl at his old alpha. Alpha Davis had always been an asshole, but Chris had never realized just how threatened the man felt by Kyle. He wasn't even right to have felt that, because Kyle couldn't care less about being alpha. Kyle might have postured when he'd first arrived in Green Hill because he thought it was the only way for him and the rest of their family to be safe, but he didn't want to be in charge of a bunch of people, be they wolves or tigers. He just wanted to be disgustingly happy with his mate, and now he was.

Chris had been looking for his brother, thinking they could spend time together. It had been a while since they'd done so, mostly because everything had been a mess after they'd arrived in town. Kyle had been an idiot and had tried to take the alpha position from the Green Hill pride alpha. He'd failed miserably.

Well, not miserably. He'd failed but had been glad for it because he didn't actually want to be the alpha and because he'd met his mate.

Which was who Kyle was spending time with right now.

1

Chris eyed them. They were on the couch, the TV on, but neither of them was watching. He wasn't sure what they'd been doing, but Kyle was stretched out against Dennis's side, his head tucked under Dennis's chin. His eyes were closed, and Dennis was cradling him close and watching him with a sappy expression.

It wasn't like Kyle to fall asleep in the middle of the day, especially not in a spot where anyone could see him. For a while, he'd continued acting as if he was a strong tiger shifter who could be the alpha if he wanted to, and he was—he just didn't want to be alpha. Now that he'd settled in, though, he'd relaxed and looked at home here.

Chris supposed he was. Kyle's father was the previous alpha of the pride, and while the man was gone, the place kind of was Kyle's ancestral home. But it had more to do with the fact that Kyle found his mate here than who his father was. Either way, Kyle had settled in, and it was like he'd always been here. He belonged.

Something Chris couldn't say about himself.

He moved back into the hallway, not wanting to bother Dennis and Kyle. Dennis hadn't noticed him yet, and he didn't want to be seen at all. Dennis would insist on waking up Kyle, and that wasn't what Chris wanted, even though he felt alone.

He looked right and left, but the hallway was empty. Kyle was busy, which meant Chris would have to find someone else to spend time with. He didn't have friends here, which meant he was stuck spending time with his family. Jennifer was next on his list.

It took a while to find her. She wasn't in her room or in any of the communal living areas in the house. That left the yard, but Jennifer didn't usually spend a lot of time outside during fall and winter. She disliked the cold and rain.

But that was where Chris found her. It was the middle of

November, and Jennifer was outside, willingly jumping in puddles. Chris watched her from the kitchen back door, wondering when his sister had been kidnapped by aliens and replaced by a pod person. There was no way this was the sister he'd grown up with.

Yet it was. There weren't many wolves in the Green Hill pride. In fact, there were only three of them — Chris, Jennifer, and their grandfather.

Chris swallowed as he watched his sister pounce on a massive tiger. He didn't recognize the tiger, but if he had to guess, it was Annabelle. She and Jennifer had become close friends, which made sense since Annabelle was Dennis's sister, and Dennis was Kyle's mate. They were like a big happy family.

Except for Chris.

He huffed and turned away from the back door. Kyle was busy with Dennis, and Jennifer was playing around with Annabelle. What was Chris's grandfather up to?

Chris had seen him in the library earlier, so that was where he headed. Sure enough, his grandfather was still there, reading a book by the fireplace. It was cozy, and Chris was tempted to shift into his wolf form and curl up by his grandfather's feet. He didn't want to bother him, though. If Chris did that, his grandpa would get worried, and Chris didn't want that.

His grandfather looked peaceful. He hadn't had an easy life, especially after losing his only daughter. Chris remembered how much his grandfather had loved her. Their life had been a mess because she'd refused to marry the alpha, but they'd been happy until she died.

That seemed to be when everything had gone to shit. The pack had tolerated them before, but after she passed away, everyone had kept as much distance from them as they could. Kyle had been angry, but Chris didn't blame them. They'd known the alpha would do something to them, and he had.

He'd kicked Kyle out.

Chris suspected that if the alpha could've gotten away with it, he would've kicked him and Jennifer out, too. He'd hated that the woman he wanted hadn't wanted him, and he'd gotten his revenge on her children after she passed away. He hadn't been able to do anything about Jennifer and Chris because they were wolves, but he had to have known that if he kicked Kyle out, the rest of his family would follow.

They had, and now here they were, sharing a house with a bunch of tiger shifters. They were only the tip of the iceberg. In the weeks since they'd moved there, Chris had been told about how both the alpha and the beta of the pride were bear shifters, about a fainting goat shifter and his friends, two deer shifters. There were Nix hanging around, and all of that mixed to form a pride that Chris had never suspected could exist. He still wasn't sure he understood how everyone could be so welcoming to people who weren't like them and who didn't belong, but that was his upbringing. His mother and his grandfather had done their best, but their alpha had been an asshole who'd only wanted wolves in his pack, and as soon as he'd been able to get away with it, that was what he'd aimed for.

Watching his grandfather, Chris realized he didn't want to interrupt him. For once, he was having a bit of time on his own without having to worry about his grandkids. Could Chris really bother him? His grandfather would welcome him and put down his book, but Chris didn't have it in himself.

He turned and walked down the hallway. He needed to do something, but he wasn't sure what. He should probably try making friends among the pride members, but he felt like an intruder. Everyone knew everyone, and he was a newcomer.

So the living room was out, as was the kitchen and the rest of the house. The yard and forest outside were out, too, because Jennifer was there. That only left the small town of

Green Hill.

And Chris could do with a nice coffee.

Luckily, when they'd moved, he'd brought his car. That meant he didn't have to wait for anyone or ask permission to leave the house. He just had to go up to his bedroom, grab the keys and his jacket, and leave the house.

He had the codes to the gate and the alarm, which should probably help him feel like he really was a pride member, but it was still awkward. He was relieved when he left the house behind, even though, technically, it was his home.

He'd get used to it. He'd always been a bit of a loner, mostly because people in his pack tended to stay away from him because of his family. He'd been fine with that, but it meant he didn't know how to make friends. Should he just go up to people and start talking to them? That thought made him want to run the other way, so probably not.

Well, he could think about it while he got coffee. Maybe he'd even be generous and bring back something for the rest of his family. Jennifer had taken a liking to Dennis's banana donuts, so Chris could check if they still had some at the bakery before going home.

But first, coffee.

Drake wasn't new to blind dates. In fact, a lot of dates he'd recently been on were blind dates. His friends, family, and colleagues wanted him to be paired off as much as he did, and they never missed an opportunity to help.

Right now, he wished Linda *had* missed the opportunity.

He wasn't sure what she'd been thinking, but the guy sitting in front of him was awful. He was dressed well and looked clean, and when he'd walked in, Drake had been impressed, but not for long. The man's personality was awful. If Drake could get away with it, he'd run out the door without looking back.

"Do you know how much sugar is in that coffee?" Karl asked, leaning closer to Drake.

Drake had been puzzled when Karl had dragged his chair to his side of the table instead of sitting in front of him like anyone else would have. It was easier to get to know each other when you could look each other in the eyes, but Karl didn't seem to think so.

Or maybe he was trying to get to know Drake in an entirely different way that involved getting his hands on him.

Karl squeezed Drake's knee, and Drake jerked his leg away. He bumped into one of the legs of the table, wincing when pain shot through his knee.

Karl didn't seem bothered. He wasn't touching Drake anymore, but that didn't stop him from leaning into his personal space.

"All that sugar is going to kill you."

Drake took a sip of his caramel latte, which was the only thing keeping him here at the moment. It was also the only thing keeping him from screaming at Karl to give him space. He didn't want to alarm the people in the coffee shop, so it was better if he continued sipping and staying as far away from Karl as possible.

"Sugar doesn't kill anyone," Drake muttered.

"You can't be serious. Do you know how many people in this country are obese?"

"I'm not," Drake pointed out. He might be a little fluffy and slightly overweight, but not that much.

Karl looked him up and down. "Well, you could lose some weight. I could help you. We could have you in shape in just a few months. Imagine how much prettier you'd be."

Karl didn't seem to find Drake repulsive, no matter what he was saying. He stretched out his arm again, squeezing Drake's thigh this time.

Drake made a sound deep in his throat that made him sound like he was dying. Maybe part of him was. His soul certainly felt like it was withering, although that possibly was to get away from Karl.

Drake looked up as he moved away from Karl, inadvertently making eye contact with the woman sitting at the table next to them. She grimaced, and while Drake was grateful for the silent support, there was unfortunately nothing she could do for him. He was the only one who could do anything about this, but it was always hard for him to tell people to fuck off. He wanted everyone to be happy, even if it meant that he wasn't.

His obsession with pleasing people was going to be the death of him.

"I'm fine," he muttered.

He could feel Karl's gaze on him as intensely as if Karl were touching him, which made him want to scream.

"You really are," Karl said with a smirk. "How about you show me how fine you are in a more private setting? Are you done with your coffee?"

Drake had been taking a sip, and it went down the wrong way. He coughed, relieved that he wasn't spraying caramel latte everywhere. That might have been the best way to get rid of Karl, though. Maybe Drake could try drowning in his latte a second time if it meant kicking Karl to the curb.

"We just met fifteen minutes ago," he pointed out.

Karl gave him a toothy smile. "So? People have sex when they barely know each other, and we've been talking for fifteen minutes."

"What did Linda tell you I was looking for?" There was no way she would've wanted Drake to meet with Karl if Karl had behaved like this. She hadn't said much about Karl, but she'd made it sound like he was a nice person, which was the opposite of the guy sitting next to Drake.

"She just mentioned a colleague. I asked to see a picture, and when I said you were hot, I decided we should go on a date."

"You decided?"

"I mean, Linda is nice, but she was talking about love and relationships. We both know that's not why we're here."

Karl had the balls to wink. Drake stared at him, unable to comprehend what was happening. He wasn't even sure *what* was happening. He just knew he wanted to get as far away from Karl as he could, as quickly as possible. "Actually, it *is* why I'm here," he said. "I'm looking for a relationship, not a one-night stand." Or a one-afternoon stand. There was no way he was sleeping with Karl, though. He'd rather set himself on fire.

Karl blinked. "Who would want a relationship with you?"

Drake did *not* want to know what that meant. He didn't care. Karl's opinion didn't matter, and it never would, because Karl was an asshole.

Drake clutched his latte, knowing he'd reached the end of his patience—and he had a lot of it. He got to his feet, ignoring the startled way Karl looked at him. "I have to go."

"Already? But we've just started talking, and we haven't even gotten to the best part of the date yet."

"Like I said, I'm not looking for whatever *you* are looking for. I want to get to know someone, fall in love, and have a relationship that will last the rest of my life. It's clear we're not looking for the same thing, so it's probably for the best if we end the date before it can get any more serious." There was no way in hell anything would ever be serious between Drake and Karl, but even though Drake was dumping Karl, he didn't want to be rude to him.

Maybe he should be, because Karl caught his wrist and pulled as if he wanted Drake to sit again.

"If you really want a relationship, we can discuss it," he

tried. "There will be boundaries, though."

Drake was tempted to stay, because he was curious about what boundaries Karl was talking about. Karl was still holding his wrist, though, and the sensation of their skin touching made Drake want to rush home and shower. Karl's hand was perfectly warm and dry, but it still felt slimy.

"No, thank you."

Karl frowned as if he didn't understand why Drake was saying no. "I'm offering you what you want. Why are you saying no?"

Drake should tell Karl it was because he was a creepy asshole, but he didn't have it in him. He looked around the coffee shop, desperate to find a way out of the situation without making it messier. He didn't know anyone here, which meant that if he wanted to get away from Karl, he'd have to act as if he did. Hopefully, whoever he latched onto would go along with it and not demand that Drake ask him what the fuck was happening and who he was.

The coffee shop door opened, catching Drake's attention. A tall man came in, and for a moment, the world stopped. He was on the thin side, lanky, with fluffy brown hair and curious eyes. He looked around the coffee shop as if he'd never been in one, and for a second, Drake couldn't breathe.

Then Karl squeezed his wrist again, and Drake snatched his hand away. "I'm sorry. I need to go."

"What are you talking about? Sit down, Drake. We're still on our date, and I'm not done with you."

Karl clearly thought Drake was going to go along with this, but Drake wouldn't stick around even if someone offered him a million dollars. "I'll see you soon," he promised Karl, even though he had no intention of seeing him ever again if he could avoid it.

He rushed toward the man who'd walked in, and as soon as he was close enough, he grabbed the man's arm and squeezed. The man looked down at him, so Drake quickly explained, "Just go along with it, please. Free me from this awful blind date." He sucked in a breath and almost stumbled back.

What were the odds of him latching onto his mate?

Chris had no idea what was happening, but that was par for the course recently. He had no idea what was happening most of the time.

But it was the first time someone latched onto him like an octopus. Maybe the guy was an octopus shifter. Chris had no way to know, and he didn't think he wanted to find out.

The man who'd latched onto him had wrapped both arms around Chris's arm, almost spilling his coffee on Chris's jacket. Chris was glad the guy had realized what he was doing before making a mess and that he'd been careful, but that still didn't explain what was happening.

He shook his arm, but the man continued staring up at him with wide eyes.

Chris understood why seconds later.

The air was heavy with the scent of coffee and people, but under all of that — or maybe above it because it was the only thing Chris could smell now — was the scent of Chris's mate. There was no doubt in Chris's mind that the scent came from the man hanging on to him, and he didn't know what to do with that revelation.

"What's happening?" he asked, but he wasn't sure what he was asking. Was he asking the guy to confirm they were mates? Was he asking for an explanation as to why the guy had latched onto him?

"That's what I'd like to know," a cool voice said.

Chris turned to find a blond man wearing a suit glaring at him. The man was handsome, with his hair slickly parted and a square jaw, but there was a coldness in his eyes that told

Chris he didn't want anything to do with the guy.

To be fair, he wasn't sure he wanted anything to do with his mate, either. He still had no fucking idea what was happening.

"I'm sorry," Drake said. "He's a friend of a friend, and he needs my help."

"What?" the snotty blond man asked.

Normally, Chris would stay out of whatever this was, but he didn't like the blond. "I do need his help," he confirmed.

His mate blinked up at him and smiled.

It went straight to Chris's heart, making it race in his chest. He'd just met his mate.

The thought was enough to calm him down and freak him out at the same time. What was he supposed to do with a mate? He'd barely ever had relationships. He was only twenty-eight, which was young for a shifter.

He should have expected to meet his mate, considering the mess the rest of his life was. Of course this was when he'd meet the guy.

He didn't know what to do with the man, but it was clear that his mate wanted nothing to do with the blond, and Chris agreed.

He gently shook off his mate and wrapped his arm around his shoulders. His mate squeaked, but he leaned closer almost instantly.

The blond didn't seem happy. "What are you doing?" he demanded to know. "You're on a date with me. Who is this guy, and why is he holding you like that?"

"Like he said, I'm a friend of a friend," Chris said with more patience than he felt. "We talked a bit on the phone, but we'd never met. We would've realized we're mates sooner if we had."

Chris's mate sucked in a breath while the blond continued staring. Normally, that would be enough to get anyone to step back, but clearly, Chris had found the one asshole who didn't seem to care that someone had met their mate.

"I don't believe you."

"Do I look like I care what you believe? Because I don't. He's my mate, and that's that." Chris hoped he wouldn't regret announcing that in the middle of the coffee shop. He didn't think any of the tiger shifters from the pride were here, but it wasn't like he knew all of them, and even those he did know, he might not recognize. He hadn't been in Green Hill long enough to know people by sight.

"He's right," Chris's mate said,

Chris really wished he could get his name. It would look weird since they were supposed to know each other, though.

"I'm really sorry," Chris's mate continued. "I didn't expect him to be my mate, but he is, and I'm sure you can understand that means that our date is over."

Chris wanted to ask his mate what he'd been thinking dating this guy, but now wasn't the moment to do that, either. He was starting to have a list of questions, though, and he hoped to get answers soon.

He didn't know what he wanted yet, but he would have time to find out. Chris's first instinct was to push away his mate and close in on himself, but this wasn't just a guy. This wasn't someone he could abandon, and he didn't *want* to abandon his mate.

That was the only thing he was sure of. Everything else, he had no idea how to deal with.

"You're here with me," the blond insisted.

How much trouble would Chris be in if he shifted in the middle of the coffee shop and tore the man's suit off him? Would he risk getting kicked out of the pride? Or would the alpha find it funny? Chris would definitely find it funny, but that didn't mean Gal would be on board, so he decided to keep his wolf under control.

For now.

"I think we can both admit that the date wasn't going well," Chris's mate softly said. "I'm really sorry, Karl. I don't want to hurt you, but I wanted to leave even before I bumped into my mate. It wouldn't have worked between us."

To Chris's astonishment, Karl actually reached out to grab his mate's wrist. He pulled, and since neither Chris nor his mate had expected it, Chris's mate stumbled forward.

Chris caught him around the waist, and for a moment, he and Karl were engaged in a tug-of-war. Chris didn't think his mate wanted to go with Karl. He'd been trying to put distance between them, but Karl didn't take no for an answer. He was also touching Chris's mate, which didn't make Chris and his wolf happy.

He growled and showed Karl his teeth. He didn't have fangs in his human form, but considering the growl, he was pretty sure Karl would understand he was a shifter and that he was ready to kick his ass for touching his mate.

Chris's mate snatched his hand away from Karl and pressed closer to Chris. Chris hadn't let go of him, and he pulled him back, wanting to make sure Karl wouldn't be able to touch him again.

"I thought you were better than this, Drake," Karl said.

Chris snorted. "Better than what? This was your first date, and he found his mate. What do you expect him to do? Finish his date with you and ignore me?"

"That would be the right thing to do," Karl said.

Chris couldn't believe it. Actually, he *could* believe it, but he was still surprised at how stupid some people could be. "I'm not letting my mate continue his date with you, especially because he told you he didn't want to." Chris looked down at Drake, happy to have a name and even happier to get Drake out of there. "Do you need to get anything?"

Drake shook his head. He'd set his drink on the counter

earlier and gestured at it now. "I already got coffee. I'm set."

Chris snatched the coffee from the counter and nodded. "All right. Let's go, then."

"You can't just walk out on me," Karl complained.

"Just let it go, Karl," Drake said. "We weren't meant to be."

When Chris steered Drake toward the door, Drake came easily. Chris was still relieved they could leave, since everyone was staring at them. He rushed his mate out of the coffee shop, not minding at all that he hadn't gotten anything to drink. He didn't care about that. He just cared about Drake.

The door closed behind them, and for a moment, Chris just stared ahead. He had his mate, so now what? What did he do with him? What did he say?

And was there a way to ignore the panic swelling in his chest?

Drake didn't know what to say. He was relieved and grateful that his mate had gotten him out of the coffee shop and away from Karl, over the moon happy that he'd found his mate, and overwhelmed by all of it.

He took a sip of his coffee because his mouth was dry but wrinkled his nose when he found it cold. He'd wasted so much time with Karl that his coffee had gotten cold, dammit.

But that didn't matter, because he had something more important to focus on. He turned to his mate, trying to choose the one question he should ask first. "What's your name?"

His mate blinked down at him. He was taller than Drake, which Drake loved. "Christopher. Most people call me Chris."

Drake nodded. "Do you *want* me to call you Chris?"

"Yeah."

"Chris it is, then. I'm Drake."

"I know. I heard your date call you that. He's still staring, by the way."

At the reminder that Karl was still in the coffee shop, Drake looked up. Sure enough, Karl was glaring at him and Chris. "Do you think we could walk away? I don't really care about him, but I don't feel comfortable with him glaring a hole in my forehead."

Chris gestured down the sidewalk.

It was clear that now that they were away from Karl, he was a bit more hesitant, but that was okay. Drake didn't have a problem taking the lead.

For years, he'd yearned to meet his mate. He'd always wanted to have that kind of relationship, that kind of person in his life. It had gotten worse after his friend Dennis had met his mate, and he'd seen how happy Dennis and Kyle were. He'd wanted the same thing, and now, he could have it.

Drake bounced on the balls of his feet, grabbed Chris's hand, and pulled him down the sidewalk. "I have to thank you for stepping in when you did," he said. "Karl was a blind date organized by one of my colleagues, but as much as I love Linda, I'm going to have to yell at her when I see her tomorrow. He was awful. I don't know why she thought he'd be a good fit for me, but it almost feels as if he threatened her into organizing this date, you know? It's not like her to ignore the signs. She wants me to be happy, and she had to know I wouldn't be happy with Karl."

Drake looked up to see that Chris was blinking at him. He understood why. He tended to overshare and talk too fast and too much when he was excited, and there was nothing more exciting than finding his mate. It was a lot for people who weren't used to it, though.

"I'm sorry," he quickly said. "Feel free to tell me to shut up if it's too much for you, but I'm excited. I didn't think I'd meet my mate while I was on a blind date with an asshole, but I couldn't have asked for anyone better than you to rescue me.

I'm just sorry you didn't have the opportunity to get something to drink. We could go back when Karl leaves if you want."

"I'm fine," Chris said with a grunt.

That was all Drake got out of him. He wanted to draw Chris out of his shell, but that seemed to be easier said than done. Drake had to be careful, because he was known for steamrolling people. He talked a lot and generally took over conversations, but that wasn't something he wanted to do right now.

Once they were far enough away from the coffee shop, he slowed down, but he didn't let go of Chris's hand.

Chris didn't, either.

Drake beamed. They were already holding hands.

"So, as I said earlier, I'm Drake," he explained. "I'm a shifter, which you probably already know from the smell. I'm pretty sure you're a wolf shifter, but I'm not. I'm an aardwolf shifter."

Chris blinked again. "I've never heard of that."

Drake shrugged. He wasn't offended, because a lot of people had never heard of it. Most humans expected shifters to be lions, tigers, wolves, or bears. That was what most shifters were in books and movies. They never considered smaller shifters that were less impressive, so most people didn't, either. "I guess you can call me a small hyena, or as some say, the hyena's weird cousin. Obviously I'm not actually one, but I look similar, just smaller. I don't laugh, though."

Chris nodded, but he looked more like he was going along with whatever Drake was saying than like he understood what was happening. It was sweet and made Drake want to cuddle him. He didn't, because they were in public and he didn't know if Chris would like that, but he made a mental note to ask once they were in a more private setting. He couldn't wait to cuddle his mate.

"Are you a wolf, then?" Drake asked since Chris wasn't volunteering any kind of information.

Chris nodded curtly. "I am. Is that a problem?"

"Why would it be a problem?" Drake asked with a frown. "I mean, it's not like either of us can do anything about what kind of shifter we are. You're a wolf, and I'm an aardwolf. That's never going to change."

"No, it's not," Chris murmured.

Drake wished he could read his mate's mind. He desperately wanted to know what Chris was thinking about. Chris looked confused, which would be normal even if they weren't mates because that was how most people felt when they were with Drake. The only people who didn't tease Drake for it were his best friends, but they weren't here right now.

They knew how much he'd wanted to meet his mate. He'd been talking their ears off for years, and it had only gotten worse after Dennis had met Kyle. They would have a field day with this, but Drake couldn't find it in himself to care. He'd met his mate, and nothing could bring him down from the high of that.

"Anyway, I moved to Green Hill a few years ago," Drake explained. "I don't think I've ever seen you around, though. Does that mean you're new here, too?"

Chris cleared his throat. "I just moved here with my family." He looked down at their hands, which were still linked. He wiggled his fingers as if he wanted Drake to let go.

Even though Drake didn't want to, he did. The last thing he wanted was for Chris to be uncomfortable with him. They were going to spend decades together. They needed to be comfortable around each other, and that had to start right from the beginning.

"That sounds great," Drake said. "You have siblings? Who else moved with you?"

"My grandfather, my brother, and my sister." Chris shook

his head. "Look, Drake, I'm sure you're a very nice guy, but I have to go."

Drake frowned. "Oh, you're busy. Of course. Well, I can give you my number, or you can give me yours, and we can text. That way, we'll have each other's number."

Drake fumbled with his jacket to get his phone out, unlocked it, and raised it toward Chris. He frowned harder when he realized that Chris had stepped away, putting more distance between them.

"Chris?" he asked.

Chris shook his head. "I'm sorry. I have to go."

"That's fine, but give me your number first. That way, we can get in touch."

Chris's foot caught on a welcome mat in front of a store. He stumbled back and quickly turned to check what he'd stepped on. Drake rushed forward to help him if he needed to, but Chris turned around and rushed away, leaving Drake standing like an idiot in the middle of the sidewalk.

Had his mate just run away from him?

Drake sighed and put his phone back into his pocket. He knew he should've kept his mouth shut. He'd apologized for talking so much, but he knew how much people were bothered by it anyway. He should have done a better job keeping himself under control, but he'd been so excited, and he hadn't thought his mate, of all people, would have a problem with that.

It looked like he was wrong.

CHAPTER TWO

Chris had never realized that he could panic for such a long time, but he'd been freaking out over Drake ever since he'd met him yesterday, and he still didn't know what to do. He'd been hiding in his bedroom, feeling like a child but unable to leave his bed.

Drake was his mate, but he didn't know what to do. The only thing he did know was that Drake wouldn't find him in his bedroom, which was why he was there. Unfortunately for him, he'd eaten all the snacks he'd kept there, which meant that if he wanted to eat, he'd have to leave the safety of his bed.

He wasn't looking forward to it. For some reason, he expected Drake to jump out from behind the couch or something and surprise him. He didn't know why Drake would do that or how he'd be at the pride house, but when he thought about it, he started freaking out all over again, and there was only one way to deal with that.

Burying deeper in his bed.

It wasn't like anyone would notice, anyway. No one had realized he wasn't at dinner yesterday or at breakfast this morning. Kyle was focused on Dennis and their new relationship, while Jennifer had made a bunch of friends and barely even thought of Chris at this point. Their grandfather might have noticed that Chris wasn't around, but he was busy relaxing and finally not feeling like he was responsible for his grandkids' well-being, and Chris didn't want to take that away from him.

He pushed the blankets away from his face and stared at the ceiling. Why was he hiding? Why did he feel so panicked at the thought of being with his mate? It wasn't like Drake had done anything to him. They barely knew each other, but they were mates, which meant they were supposed to work well together. Chris had a hard time believing it, but he'd seen bonded couples together, and he knew that was true. They really did belong together.

Like he belonged with Drake.

He sucked in a breath and squeezed his eyes shut. Why was he so afraid of this? Just yesterday, he'd been bemoaning the fact that he was the only one who felt like he didn't belong here. He was the only one who didn't have a mate, new friends, or an entire library to read.

Well, he had a mate now. He just needed to find Drake, talk to him, and see where they both stood. Surely he could do that.

He wasn't sure.

When he thought about doing it, he panicked all over again. He might not understand why he felt that way, but he did feel like the only way out of this would be to run away, and he couldn't ignore that.

A knock on his door startled him. He listened for a moment, trying to figure out who it was, but he couldn't. He wasn't sure he wanted to find out, but at the same time, they might worry about him and go to the alpha. Chris still wasn't sure what he thought of Gal, and he'd rather avoid annoying the bear shifter.

He crawled out of bed and went to open. There was a second knock before he could reach the door, and he rolled his eyes. "I'm coming," he yelled. He looked around the room, but it was too messy for him to be able to do anything about it now. Besides, it was probably someone from his family, and they were used to him being messy.

Sure enough, he found Jennifer standing in the hallway. She looked him up and down and cocked her head, silently asking a question.

Chris ignored her. "What?"

"Is that a way to greet your favorite sister?"

"You're my only sister, and yet you're still not my favorite."

She pushed Chris, and he stumbled back, which gave her enough space to walk into the bedroom. She closed the door and leaned against it as if she was afraid that Chris would run away if she didn't.

He might.

"What?" he asked again.

"You weren't at dinner yesterday."

"I'm surprised you managed to look away from Annabelle long enough to notice that."

Jennifer blinked. "What are you talking about?"

"Nothing." Chris didn't want Jennifer to feel guilty or like she shouldn't be having fun with her friends. This was Chris's problem, not hers. It wasn't her fault that he was an introvert who would rather have his teeth pulled than casually talk to people. It made making friends almost impossible, and that was when he didn't isolate himself.

"You also weren't at breakfast this morning," Jennifer pushed. "It's weird, because you're always the first in line when it comes to eating. Unless you were out?"

Chris opened his arms, gesturing to himself. "Does it look like I've been out?" He was wearing a pair of pajama pants and a t-shirt with holes at the neckline.

"With you, I'm never sure. It looks like you're in your pajamas, but it could also be something you'd wear to the grocery store."

"Why did I let you in again?"

"You didn't. I came in because I was worried about you."

Her expression softened. "What is it? I know we're not spending as much time together as we used to, but it doesn't mean I don't care. You know that if there's anything I can do, I want to help you. You just need to talk to me."

For a moment, Chris thought about telling her everything. What would she say if he did? She'd be happy for him, and she wouldn't understand why he was so hesitant. He didn't understand it himself. He wanted to belong, and having a mate in town would help with that, yet thinking of Drake made him panic. What was it about him that made Chris simultaneously want him and want to run away from him?

"Chris?" Jennifer asked softly.

Chris shook his head. "I'm fine. I don't need to talk to you or to anyone else."

"It doesn't look like it. I think something happened yesterday, but I can't help if you don't tell me. We tell each other everything."

"That was before, Jen. Things have changed since we arrived here. *You've* changed."

Her expression fell, making Chris feel like an asshole. He wanted to take back the words, but they were true. Jennifer *had* changed. It was for the best, since now she had a future, friends, and people who would support her through everything and didn't care about who her parents were. Chris wanted that for her, but he wasn't sure where that left him.

"I'm sorry," she murmured.

"You don't need to be. This is why we moved, isn't it? So we could all have a better life. That's what you're building. I want you to continue doing so, and you shouldn't have to worry about your brother as you do."

She put her hands on her hips. "You're my baby brother. Do you really think I could stop worrying about you?"

"Gosh, I hope so, because I've had enough of you calling me your baby brother. I'm twenty-eight."

"A baby."

Chris grabbed one of his shoes from the floor and threw it at her. She laughed and jumped out of the way, letting it land against the wall. Hopefully, it hadn't gotten scuffed. That didn't stop Chris from threatening Jennifer with his second shoe.

She raised her hands. "Fine. No need to assault me with a deadly weapon."

"It's a shoe," Chris complained.

"Exactly. A deadly weapon."

He was tempted to throw the shoe at her, but instead, he dumped it back where he'd found it and flopped on the bed.

"Look, I'm not going to push, even though I can see that something's happening," Jennifer said as she stepped closer and squeezed Chris's shoulder. "I'm sure you'll talk to us once you feel ready. I just want you to know that whatever happens, I'm here for you. You're my family, first and fore-most. I love that the pride welcomed us, and I hope we'll never have to leave, but if I have to choose between them and you, there's no competition."

Chris reached up and squeezed his sister's shoulder. "You're sure about that?"

"More sure than anything else in my life. I mean, I love this place and Annabelle and everyone else, so of course I hope we can stay, but if we can't, I'm coming with you."

Chris pulled his sister closer, grinning when she yelped and grabbed his shoulders for balance. He hugged her, bury-ing his face against her stomach like he did when he was younger. She was only a few years older than him, but they'd always been close.

Chris prayed that would never change.

Drake didn't know anything about Chris. That was a

problem.

It meant he had no idea where to find Chris. He didn't even know if Chris lived in Green Hill proper or outside of it. He'd mentioned that he'd recently moved here with his family, but unfortunately, that didn't help Drake locate him.

He groaned and bumped his head against the table. He was having lunch at the coffee shop, part of him hoping he'd find Chris here, but he was nowhere to be seen. Drake hadn't actually expected him to be, but he'd hoped.

How did one find someone they knew nothing about? It wasn't like Drake could walk the streets of Green Hill screaming for Chris. Eventually Chris might hear him, and even if he didn't, he'd definitely hear all the gossip, but it wasn't how Drake wanted to start things between them.

He tapped his fingertips on the table before taking a sip of coffee. He'd have to get back to work soon, but since he'd spent his entire half-hour thinking about Chris and not coming up with any solution, maybe it wasn't a bad thing. Maybe he needed to distract himself from Chris and the fact that he was somewhere out there, living in town, and there was a chance that Drake would never find him.

He shook his head. He couldn't think that way. Green Hill was a small town, and while a lot of people lived here, it wasn't so big that Drake couldn't find a newcomer like Chris. He suspected that he'd have to ask around and find the right people who could tell him where Chris and his family were. It felt a bit like an invasion of privacy, especially since Chris had left before he could give Drake his number, but Drake needed to know.

Why had Chris run away? Why had he looked like he'd rather die than have a mate?

It hurt to think that. Drake had been looking for his mate for a long time, possibly ever since he'd learned what mates were. He'd finally found him, but he might have ruined everything by being himself.

Where did that leave him?

Well, he knew that if Chris ever gave him a second chance, he'd make sure not to be himself. That was usually why people ran, and he didn't want Chris to run.

So being himself was out. Drake would have to keep quiet, give Chris space to speak, and listen to him. That wouldn't be a hardship, because he was interested in Chris and wanted to find out as much as he could about him, but usually, he talked a lot. He liked talking to people about his experiences because he felt it made him more relatable.

How many people could relate to a man dumped by his mate on the sidewalk without one word of explanation?

He stared at his phone. He hadn't told anyone about Chris yet, and part of him wanted to keep all of it a secret. If he didn't tell his friends, he wouldn't have to admit that Chris had run away from him. He wouldn't have to tell them how horrible it must have been for Chris to realize that they were mates. It was clear he didn't want to spend the rest of his life with Drake, which Drake supposed was fine. It wasn't like he could force anyone to be with him, let alone his mate.

It wasn't fine. It was so painful that it broke his heart. There was only one explanation for Chris running, and it was that he didn't want Drake. Clearly, Chris hadn't had the courage to tell him face-to-face, so instead, he'd left him behind.

And that left Drake picking through the shards of what remained of his heart, trying to find a new reason to live.

He took another sip of coffee and admitted that he was being dramatic. It wasn't like he was dying or anything. It might feel like that for a bit, but Drake had had boyfriends before Chris, and if Chris rejected him, he'd have boyfriends after him, too.

He just didn't want to.

He hesitated. He wasn't sure he wanted to tell anyone

about the rejection, but he had friends, and they'd be happy to find out he'd met his mate — before turning angry and threatening Chris when Drake told them he'd run. A few of them would probably offer to go get him and drag him back, which Drake would be tempted to accept if he knew where to find him.

He shook his head and unlocked his phone. He had a group text with Dennis, Taylor, and Jacob. He pulled that up, then hesitated, trying to think of what to write.

I didn't tell you what happened yesterday, he typed and sent.

Jacob's three dots started dancing on the screen. Drake waited for his answer to come through, rolling his eyes when it did. *A squirrel stole your donut?*

Drake's fingers flew on the screen. *That happened* one *time. There's no need for you to bring it up every time we text.*

What would be the fun in that? Jacob answered.

And where would be the fun of not telling you that I met my mate? There. Drake might as well come clean and tell his friends everything.

More dots started dancing on the screen. Jacob wasn't the only one answering, and Drake leaned back, waiting. He already knew his friends would have something to say, which was fine because it was why he was reaching out to them. He needed advice.

Of the four of them, only Dennis had a mate, and the relationship was recent. He might not be able to tell Drake much, but maybe Drake would be lucky. Maybe it was a way for him to locate his mate when they weren't bonded yet.

Congratulations! Taylor texted. Jacob texted the same seconds later.

What he said, Dennis texted. *When were you going to tell us?*

Gosh, Drake wanted to hug the three of them. He would if they were here, but it felt easier to tell them this through texts. Usually Drake preferred texts, maybe emails, but right now, he wished he had his friends here so he could hug them.

It only happened yesterday, and I'm still confused, Drake admitted.

Finding your mate will do that to you.

It's not fair, Jacob complained.

You'll find your mate, too, eventually, Drake told him. *But I'm really confused, and I don't know anything about him, and I don't know how to find him.*

Where are you? Dennis asked.

Coffee shop. I still have about ten minutes before I have to go back to work.

Dennis didn't answer. In fact, none of the three texted again, leaving Drake to stare at his phone, hoping they would. He'd just told them he'd met his mate. Surely they were happy for him? They might even throw him a tiny party of four — or five if Drake ever managed to find Chris.

The coffee shop door opened, and like every time it had today, Drake looked up, hoping it was Chris. It wasn't, but it was the next best thing.

Jacob and Dennis made a beeline for him. Dennis bumped his shoulder against Jacob's, tilting his chin toward the counter. Drake could almost hear the whine coming from Jacob, but Jacob didn't argue and went up to the counter to order coffee while Dennis dropped into the chair in front of Drake.

"You met your mate," he said.

Drake nodded. "And promptly lost him. He just — left, and I don't even have his number. I don't know how to find him."

Dennis reached over the table and squeezed Drake's hand. "I don't want you to worry about any of this. Green Hill is a small town, so as long as he lives here, we'll find him. You just have to tell us everything you know about him."

"But not until I'm there, too," Jacob yelled.

Dennis grinned and raised his hand. His eyes widened when he noticed a little boy staring at him, so he wiggled his fingers at him instead of giving Jacob the middle finger like Drake suspected he'd been about to. Jacob snorted, but when the woman behind the counter called his name, he quickly turned his attention to her.

He was back in seconds, placing a coffee in front of Dennis and taking a sip of his before fixing his gaze on Drake. "Tell us about him."

"I only know a few things. His name is Chris, and he's a wolf shifter. He told me he recently moved to Green Hill with his family — his grandfather, his brother, and his sister." Neither Dennis nor Jacob said anything. Drake looked up to find both of them gaping at him. "What?"

"I believe your mate is my mate's brother," Dennis said, stunning Drake into silence.

Could it really be that easy?

Chris had been ready to throw Jennifer out of his bedroom when she first arrived, but he'd missed her, and he liked spending time with her. They both got onto the bed and watched a few episodes of the series Chris was currently obsessed with, but Jennifer wasn't really paying attention. She kept babbling about her friends and her new life, and while Chris was happy for her, he couldn't help but wonder if he would ever have that.

He knew it was his fault. He was pretty closed off, and even though he was now a pride member, he hadn't tried making friends with the people who shared a home with him. The rest of his family had settled in as if they'd always belonged, but not him.

It was just taking him more time to wrap his mind around the fact that they were here to stay and that they'd found a new home where they were safer than they ever could have been with their pack. He'd also never really had friends because of the distance most pack members had put between themselves and Chris and his family, and he wouldn't know where to start.

For now, he was fine with just his family. He would have to open up a bit, though. The thought made him uncomfortable, but he could do it.

He flopped back onto the bed once Jennifer left and wondered if he should watch another episode or if he should go downstairs for lunch. The dining room and kitchen were probably almost empty by now, so he wouldn't have to talk to too many people. He'd have to get dressed, but he supposed it would be better if he did that, anyway. Spending all day in his pajamas, buried in his bed, wasn't good.

Another knock on his door distracted him. It could be only one of two people, so he rolled his eyes as he opened it. "What?" he asked his brother.

Kyle raised a covered plate. "Is that how you talk to your favorite brother?"

Chris made grabby hands. "You know, that's what Jennifer said."

"That she was your favorite brother?"

"That she's my favorite sister."

"Exactly, and I'm your favorite brother."

"If you say so."

Kyle raised the plate so Chris couldn't grab it.

Chris grinned at him. He and his brother didn't always see eye to eye, but they were family, and Chris loved him. "Fine. You're my favorite brother, but only because I can say that Dennis is my favorite brother-in-law."

Kyle barked out a laugh. "We'll go with that." He handed the plate to Chris, who was relieved to see there was a napkin with a fork tucked into it on top of it. He grabbed it and uncovered the plate, smiling at the sight of mac and cheese.

He stabbed a piece of broccoli and stuffed it into his mouth, sighing in relief at the thought that he wouldn't have to go downstairs and face half the pride.

Kyle grabbed the chair by the desk and moved it so he and Chris could face each other. "So, what happened? Why are you hiding in your bedroom?"

"I'm not hiding."

Kyle gestured at the unmade bed and at Chris, probably because he was still wearing pajamas. "Really?"

"Not you, too. I just felt like spending some time in bed."

"I mean, you *are* lazy, but this isn't like you. Did something happen? Are you having trouble with some pride members?" Kyle leaned forward. "Because if you are, we can find a solution. You don't have to face that on your own."

"I don't have problems with any pride members, so put away the fangs. I'm fine." More than fine, actually. Just yesterday, Chris had been lamenting the fact that his siblings were too busy with their own lives to dedicate any attention to him, and today, both Jennifer and Kyle had visited him. It was mainly because they were worried, but Chris didn't care. They were here, talking to him. He was happy.

"As long as you're sure. This is your home, too."

Chris reached out with his leg and poked Kyle's knee with his toe. "I'm sure. Everyone's been nice, so don't worry, Papa Bear."

"I don't think that's ever going to happen. I'll always worry about you and Jennifer."

Kyle wasn't that much older since he was thirty-five, but as the eldest, he'd always taken his role as protector very seriously. Sometimes it had been annoying, but now that he was older, Chris was glad he had his brother.

At least until Kyle said, "I got an interesting text from Dennis."

Chris groaned. "I don't want to know what Dennis texts you."

"Why do you say it like that?"

"I'm scared he texts you old people sex, and I can't."

Kyle made a strangled sound. "Old people sex? Why would he do that?"

"Because you're old?"

Kyle tried to kick Chris's leg, but Chris quickly pulled them both up on the mattress and stuck his tongue out. Part of him reverted to being a kid when he was with Kyle, and while Chris didn't always like it, in this situation, he did.

"We don't text about old people sex," Kyle said. "But we do text about our brother finding his mate and not telling anyone."

Chris's stomach dropped. "What are you talking about?"

"The fact that apparently, your mate is one of Dennis's best friends."

So that was how Dennis had found out. "He knows Drake?"

"Yeah. They're together right now. Drake told his friends that he met his mate yesterday but didn't know much about him, so he couldn't find him again. When he told Dennis that his mate's name was Chris and that he'd recently moved here with his two siblings and their grandfather, Dennis knew it was too much to be a coincidence." Kyle leaned forward and placed his elbows on his knees. "What happened? You didn't tell Jennifer or me that you met your mate, and from what Dennis said, it sounds like you ran away." He hesitated. "I thought you'd be happy to meet your mate."

Chris was finished eating, so he leaned sideways and set his plate down on the dresser. "I don't know. I guess I panicked."

"Finding your mate can be a lot."

Kyle was probably the best person to talk things through with, since he and Dennis had only met recently. Kyle had panicked when he'd met Dennis, too, although he'd had a good reason to. He'd been planning to fight the Green Hill pride alpha for the position, and the fact that Dennis was a pride member had made a messy situation even messier.

But there was nothing stopping Chris from talking to Drake or taking him out on a date. There was no reason for them to stay apart. If Kyle could deal with his messiness and untangle everything, maybe Chris could do the same.

"My mate was on a date," he explained. "The other guy was an asshole. Even after I told him that Drake was my mate, he insisted that Drake had agreed to go on a date with him and that they should finish that date." It had sounded a bit like Karl was going to drag Drake to his bed, because that was what he'd expected to get out of that date. It had taken everything Chris had not to slam the guy against the nearest wall and growl at him. Maybe he should have. Karl needed to learn some respect.

"That guy doesn't matter, though. Unless they're getting serious?"

"It was a first date. A blind date."

Kyle grimaced. "Those are never fun."

"I got Drake out of the coffee shop and away from the guy, and he was fine. He's a talker, though."

"Makes sense, since you're quiet. Still, I don't get why you ran away without even giving him your number."

"Honestly? I don't know. It was just too much, and I needed some space."

"You could've had that even if you'd given him your number."

Chris scowled. "Clearly, he didn't need it because he found me anyway." What were the odds that he and his brother would end up bonded to two best friends? Well, it was a bit early for Chris to be thinking about him and Drake bonding, but still. It was in their future.

As long as they gave each other a chance, which was the opposite of what Chris had done.

Drake was still freaking out, but it was for entirely different reasons now. He'd thought there was a good chance that he'd never see his mate again, yet here he was, having just found out that his mate was the brother of Dennis's mate. What were the odds?

As soon as Dennis had realized who Chris was, he'd started texting.

Drake didn't have to ask to know who he was talking to, and he hoped this wouldn't start trouble for Chris. It was the last thing Drake wanted.

What he did want was answers. "What do you know about him?" he asked.

Dennis finally set down his phone and leaned back in his chair. "Honestly, not a lot. I know he's seven years younger than Kyle and that he's the baby of the family. They lost their mother not too long ago. The situation with their pack was complicated, and they had to move when Kyle got kicked out. Their old alpha was in love with their mother, and he never forgave her for not marrying him and for having three kids with someone who wasn't him. He tolerated the family until she died, but as soon as she did, he kicked Kyle out. Chris and Jennifer are wolf shifters like their mother and the rest of the pack, but Kyle's a tiger, and the alpha used that as an excuse. He knew that if he kicked Kyle out, his siblings would follow, and he was right. Their grandfather left, too, and they moved here because of Kyle's father."

Drake sucked in a breath. "I'm really sorry to hear that." He'd left his pack a while ago and had never regretted it, but he knew that some shifters preferred to live with their families.

He was fine without them. He didn't need an entire community of people treading on his toes or to share living spaces with them, which was one of the reasons he hadn't requested to become a pride member.

He hadn't needed the pride then, and he didn't need it now, especially since he had his best friends. Sometimes they joked about how he should become a pride member, but until now, Drake had been satisfied with his life.

But what about his mate? Chris was part of the pride. Did that mean he expected Drake to be, too? Or would he be happy to leave Drake be? Drake wasn't sure he was ready for all these very serious conversations they needed to have, but they didn't need to have them now, anyway, so he forced himself to relax.

Dennis nodded. "It hasn't been easy for them, especially since Kyle thought that the only way to get his family to safety was to become the pride's alpha, but all of that is behind us now."

"You're sure?" Jacob muttered, earning himself a scowl.

"Dennis wouldn't be with him if he thought Kyle would take the pride," Drake said.

"You're only saying that because you're related to him now."

Drake blinked. It was true. He and Kyle *were* technically related now. Drake and Chris weren't bonded yet, but there was a very good chance they would be eventually, and that made them family.

"All of that is to say that he and his family have been through a lot," Dennis said, glaring at Jacob. "It would probably be good if you were a bit careful with him initially."

"I will be. I don't want to overwhelm him."

Dennis shook his head. "I wasn't talking about you. It's just that while the family has been working hard to integrate themselves, Chris has been keeping to himself. I'm sure everything's fine and that he's just an introvert, but just in case, maybe give him time?"

"I'll give him whatever he needs." Drake meant it.

Whatever his mate needed or wanted, he just had to say the words, and Drake would try his best to provide it.

That was what mates did. They were always there for each other, always ready to help or hold or comfort. Drake had yearned for that for so long that he could hardly believe he'd finally found it. He might not know what would happen with Chris, but there was a good chance they'd end up together, which was what he wanted.

But what did Chris want? Dennis had said he was probably overwhelmed, and it made sense. He'd been kicked out of his home, had lost his mother, and even though he'd found a new home, it was still a lot. Drake knew a bit about the pride, both from when he'd looked into it when he'd first moved here and from his friends, so he knew they were boisterous and that it was always quite noisy and overwhelming.

Chris didn't need anything or anyone to overwhelm him even more. That meant Drake wouldn't be able to be himself, but that was okay. He didn't need to be as open and relaxed as he would normally be. He could hide part of himself until Chris felt more comfortable with the pride and with him. It wouldn't be easy, but Drake was ready to do pretty much anything to keep his mate happy. He wouldn't do it for anyone else, not again.

He'd always been a lot. People told him that he was too bouncy, too happy, and that he talked too much. He hyperfixated on things and talked about them twenty-four-seven for weeks at a time, annoying and boring people. He started things only not to finish them and abandon them. He still had half of a blanket he'd crocheted somewhere in his closet, but he'd never finished it, and he wouldn't do so anytime soon. because for now, he wasn't interested in crochet anymore.

But this chaos wasn't what Chris needed. He needed a mate who was calm and composed, who could be his rock in the storm that was his life right now. The fact that Chris's mate happened to be Drake didn't change any of that. Drake wanted to be what Chris needed right now, and that wasn't going to be easy, but he could do it.

He didn't have a choice.

"Drake, I can already see that you're thinking the wrong things," Jacob said, reaching over the table to squeeze Drake's free hand. "Dennis isn't saying that you can't be yourself. You tried that already, and it was a disaster, remember?"

When Drake had first arrived in town, he'd known it would be hard for him to find someone to date if he was himself, so he'd kept things as low-energy as he could. He'd started dating a guy, and they were together for almost six months, but Drake had hated most of that time. He'd liked the guy, but he'd hated who he was with him, and eventually, he'd exploded. His boyfriend had run for the hills, probably more shocked than anything, and Drake had felt he'd ruined everything all on his own.

But Chris wasn't just a boyfriend, and now that Drake knew how much work it took to hide his natural self, he could do it better. He wouldn't explode on Chris.

"He's my mate. Everything will be fine."

"I know you keep trying to convince yourself of that, and I hope everything *will* be fine, but it won't be if you're not yourself. Don't you want Chris to fall in love with you instead of a manipulated image he has of you? What do you think will happen when your personality slowly comes through and he realizes he doesn't know you?"

Drake pulled his hands away and rubbed his face. "I'll be fine. It's only going to be a few weeks, just the time for him to settle in and understand that me being his mate isn't a bad thing."

"I'm sure he already knows that being your mate isn't a bad thing."

"We only talked for, like, ten minutes. He doesn't know

anything about me beyond the fact that I was on a blind date with an asshole." Drake sucked in a breath and looked at his friends. "I don't want to mess things up, you know? This is important. He's my *mate*."

"Which is why you should be yourself. If there's one person in the world you can be yourself with, it's your mate," Dennis said gently. "That's kind of the point, and faking to be someone you're not isn't going to make things easier on you or Chris."

Not in the long run, but Drake was convinced that in the short term, Chris needed something specific that Drake couldn't give him if he was himself.

Which meant that he had to stop.

CHAPTER THREE

Chris needed to do *something*, but it was so much easier to hide in his bedroom. Did that make him a coward? Possibly, but right now, he didn't care.

He didn't feel at home anywhere except in his bedroom. Even that was a bit strange, because it was much bigger than what he was used to and much emptier since he hadn't been able to bring most of his things along. It was also odd to always hear people around the house laughing and talking, or even only walking down the hallway outside the door. Chris felt like everything was changing — everything *was* — and he didn't know how to deal with that.

He definitely didn't know what to do with Drake. What was he supposed to tell him? How was he supposed to explain that he'd run away from his mate, and he didn't even know why? That he panicked at the thought of having to face him and talk to him?

He buried his face into his pillow and groaned. He wanted to scream, but he didn't dare. He was pretty sure that his siblings would rush into the room and use his screaming as an excuse to drag him out. He hadn't talked to them since a few days ago, and he was fine with that. He knew they loved him and that they'd support him, whatever he wanted. The problem was that he didn't know what he wanted.

He rolled to his back, hugged his pillow to his chest, and stared at the ceiling. Actually, he did know what he wanted. He wanted to go home to the pack, to a time when his mother had been alive. He wanted his old life back.

He would never get it. He had to make his peace with that, and most of the time, he felt he had, but meeting Drake had sent him into a downward spiral that he wasn't sure how to recover from. Hiding in his bedroom was easier and less messy than whatever else Chris would be able to do. Even though he wouldn't be able to do this forever, for now, it helped.

It wasn't just Drake that he needed to deal with, though. Gal had been nice and had given him and his family time to get used to living with the pride, but he wouldn't support them for the rest of their lives. The pride would always be there for them, possibly in a way the pack had never been, but they needed to contribute. That meant they had to find jobs and become productive members of the pride.

Chris snorted. He freaked out at the thought of leaving this bedroom. How was he supposed to find a job?

He would. He couldn't afford for Gal to regret welcoming him into the pride. It would be horrifying if the alpha decided to kick him out and keep the rest of his family. Not that Chris wouldn't deserve it, since he hadn't made an effort to truly become a member of the pride, but he wouldn't survive leaving his family behind. Even if it was only to move to Green Hill proper, he couldn't let it happen.

So where did he start?

He grabbed his phone to make a list. The first item was easy — he had to take a shower and get dressed. He'd been living in his pajamas for days, and while he did shower and change every day, he still wore pajamas.

The second item on the list should be to leave the bedroom. He wasn't sure he was ready for a meal with the rest of the pride, but he could visit the kitchen when most people were at work in the morning and grab some food, maybe even have a stilted conversation with the cooks.

That wouldn't be awkward at all.

What would be the third thing? Talking to his family? Jennifer had been texting him, but beyond telling her that he was okay, he hadn't answered. Kyle was still mostly focused on Dennis, but with Chris's mate being one of Dennis's friends, Kyle had turned some of his attention to Chris. He and Dennis wanted to know why he didn't want to see Drake, which was why Chris wasn't answering their calls or texts. If he knew why he was avoiding Drake, he wouldn't be doing it.

It wasn't like Chris didn't want to settle down with his mate and his new pride. The pride was his future, since his family had decided to stay. He wished that settling down here was as easy for him as it had been for Kyle and Jennifer, but something in him was wary at the thought of the pride being his family. He half expected them to betray him the way the pack had. The wolves had always followed the alpha's lead, which was why Chris and his family had been isolated. Chris didn't have to go through that now. His siblings definitely weren't. They were taking advantage of everything the pride had to offer, making friends and finding mates.

One of the many items on Chris's list had to be stop moping around.

It wasn't helping, only making things worse, which was the last thing Chris needed.

So showering, getting dressed, getting food, and reaching out to his siblings. It was a good start, but Chris had to stick Drake in there somewhere. He didn't know Drake well, obviously, but he'd seemed like someone who fretted, which meant that was probably what he was doing right now.

Chris would know that for sure if he reached out to Kyle and Dennis, or even better, to Drake himself, but he was scared. This felt like too much all at once, and he didn't know how to deal with it. That was why his list was a good idea. He could focus on one item at a time without being overwhelmed.

A brisk knock on his door made him jump. He rolled his head on the pillow and glared, but the person in the hallway couldn't see him, so it didn't help. There was another knock, and even though Chris didn't know who was there, he could tell they wouldn't give up.

He groaned. "What?"

"Let me in," Jennifer said.

"I don't need you to check on me. I'm fine."

He stared at the door, silently counting. He didn't even reach ten before the door swung open, and Jennifer walked in. "You don't look fine to me," she said as she took in the room.

Okay, so maybe it was a bit messier than usual, but still, there was no need for her to make that horrified face. "What do you want?"

Jennifer put her hands on her hips. "For you to stop hiding."

"I'm not hiding. I'm resting."

"You're hiding, although I'm not sure from what. Drake? The pride? Me and Kyle?"

Chris went back to staring at the ceiling. "How about all of them?"

There was a moment of silence before Jennifer sighed. "You're gonna have to explain better than that."

The bed shifted as she climbed onto it. Chris lifted the blankets, welcoming her in his warm cocoon. She settled on her back and stared at the ceiling like Chris was. She was silent, not demanding an explanation or pushing Chris into anything, but it was almost worse. The silence was heavy and pressing Chris to say something. "I don't feel like I belong," he blurted out.

"Maybe it's because you're keeping yourself apart. I swear, if the cooks hadn't assured me that you were eating, I would've thought you were starving yourself. No one's seen you around the house."

"I know it's partially my fault."

Jennifer snorted. "*Mostly* your fault." She rolled on her side. "This isn't like you. I know things aren't easy with the pride, but we have a second chance, *all* of us, but you're acting as if you don't. Why? I don't understand, Chris."

"You don't understand because you left me behind. You have your new, shiny life, and you *should* have it. You shouldn't have to worry about me."

"I thought we'd already had this conversation. I'll always worry about you, okay? I know that things have changed and that we're not each other's everything like we were at the pack, but that's not a bad thing. We both deserve more than the pack has ever given us, and the pride can be that for us. You're going to have to give it a chance, though."

"I'm not sure I know how to do that," Chris whispered.

Jennifer took his hand and squeezed hard. "I know that telling you to make friends isn't going to help. How about talking to your mate, though? If there's one person who will like you no matter what you say, it's him. He might not be a pride member, but he lives in town, and he's friends with Dennis. You don't have to bond with him, but maybe give him a chance? Allow him to take you on a date and get to know him, you know?"

Chris did know, but it wasn't any less scary.

Drake was tired, and he wasn't even doing anything tiring. His *soul* was tired.

Tired of wondering what Christopher was doing and why he was staying away. Tired of Christopher hiding. Tired of himself resisting the urge to storm the pride house, knock down Christopher's door, and make him listen to him.

That wouldn't exactly go down well, so instead of doing

what he wanted during his lunchtime, he was at the coffee shop again, staring down at his hands.

Was he sure that Chris wouldn't appreciate him knocking down his door?

He sighed. Every time he got angry, he switched from Chris to Christopher. He couldn't help but wonder how Chris would take that. He hadn't sounded like he hated his name, so it should be fine. Besides, it wasn't like he was calling Chris that to his face. It just made him feel better, almost as if he could separate Christopher from Chris. Christopher was the guy who was afraid and hiding away from Drake, while Chris would hopefully want to be Drake's mate.

Once he managed to kick *Chris* back from wherever he'd come from.

He didn't understand why Chris was freaking out so badly. It wasn't like Drake expected them to bond tomorrow or even next week. He didn't have any expectations. He wanted to get to know his mate, for them to become close, and eventually, when they were both ready, for them to bond. Unfortunately for him, it looked like it wasn't going to happen anytime soon.

That was really fine with him, but it was the only thing he was fine with in this situation. He hated that Chris was hiding, as if Drake was a serial killer running after him with a chainsaw. He hadn't even talked to him since the coffee shop. Drake had begged Dennis to give him Chris's number, but Dennis had refused. He didn't want to get in trouble with his mate's family, which was understandable, but Drake felt a bit betrayed. Dennis was one of his best friends, so shouldn't he be on his side? It wasn't like Drake was going to start blowing up Chris's phone. He just wanted to text him, maybe talk to him for a bit.

Something would have to break eventually. They couldn't continue like this, or rather, Drake didn't *want* them to continue like this. If Chris was going to reject him, he wanted to know. If Chris was doing this because he was afraid and freaking out, he wanted to know that, too. He would be happy to give Chris more time or to leave him completely alone as long as he knew what the fuck was happening.

The only way to get answers would be to talk to Chris, and Drake was done waiting. He'd given Chris time, but didn't he deserve things, too? If he wanted answers, why couldn't he get them?

He grabbed his coffee, drank what was left in the cup, and got to his feet. He'd already used almost his entire half-hour of lunch break, but he didn't care. His boss would understand that talking to his mate was more important than returning to work on time.

Hopefully.

Drake texted his boss as he walked to his car. He was nervous, and he had no idea what would come out of this, but he didn't care. As long as Chris was honest with him, he could start thinking about what came next. Maybe his life wouldn't change just yet because Chris would need more time and space. Maybe his life would change completely, and he'd feel like a different person. Either way, he didn't really care. He just wanted to know what was happening.

But what if Chris didn't want him at the house? That was a possibility that he hadn't allowed himself to think of yet. Chris could ask for Drake to be kicked out, and the alpha would have to do so because Chris was a pride member while Drake wasn't. Alphas always put their people first—when they were good alphas, anyway. From everything Drake had heard about Gal, he was a good person, so he had no doubt that Gal would support Chris.

Drake wasn't planning to upset Chris or doing anything stupid. He just wanted a conversation. Hell, he'd be fine with both of them standing in the same room, completely silent. He just needed to reassure himself that he wasn't going nuts and that he actually *had* met his mate. As the days went by, it felt more and more like he might have dreamed it, and he wasn't ready for that.

Luckily for him, it wasn't the first time he'd visited the pride. He usually came around to spend time with Dennis, Taylor, and Jacob, so he even had the gate code. He might not be a pride member, but he supposed he could consider himself an honorary tiger or something.

He parked the car as close to the house as he could, then stared ahead for a moment. He'd come all the way here, which thankfully wasn't far. What did he do now? Did he march inside, demanding to talk to his mate? Did anyone besides Dennis, Jacob, Taylor, and Kyle know about the bond? Drake didn't think Chris had told anyone else, except maybe his sister.

He wasn't taking it personally. He understood that Chris was trying to find his footing with the pride. Had he already had time to make friends? Was he talking to them at this moment, perhaps making fun of Drake and how goofy he'd been at the coffee shop?

He couldn't think like that. He didn't care what people thought of him or said behind his back.

He got out of his car and strode toward the house before he could panic and go home, but he paused at the front door. He'd come in easily through the gate, but this was different. It was still pride territory, but it was their home, and Drake didn't want anyone to think that he was invading it or something.

He knocked and took a step back. He didn't have to wait long for a little girl to open the door. She couldn't be more than four or five, and she stared at him with big brown eyes.

"Hello," he said, wondering what now.

"Do you have my food?" she asked.

"I'm afraid I don't. I'm here to see Chris."

The girl pouted. "Mommy! My food still isn't here!"

Dennis appeared from an open door on their left. He grinned at the girl and leaned down to pick her up, swung her up in the air, and made her laugh. "I think your mom's already warned you about opening the door to strangers," he said.

"I'm hungry."

Dennis winked at Drake and put the girl down. "Why don't you go to the kitchen? I'm sure someone will have a carrot for you."

The little girl beamed and ran away, leaving Drake feeling even more exhausted than a few minutes in her company warranted.

"You look good with a kid in your arms," he teased Dennis.

"You look good in the pride house."

Nope. "Seriously. You have your mate now, and I always wondered if you wanted kids."

Dennis's eyes narrowed. He'd always been able to read Drake way too easily. "Why are you here? And don't tell me it's to discuss me having kids, because I don't believe that."

"I'd like to see Chris, or at least to talk to him."

Dennis's expression turned a little sad. "That's what I thought. I don't know if he wants to see you, Drake."

"Then I'll talk to him through the door."

"And if he doesn't want to talk to you?"

"Then I'll talk *to* the door. I just need him to listen. I promise I won't do anything stupid, all right? I'm not willing to sacrifice my mate just because I want answers."

"I wouldn't say sacrifice, but Chris isn't in a good place right now."

"Then he needs his mate." It was as simple as that, even though Chris was complicating everything.

Dennis sighed and gestured at Drake to follow him as he

moved toward the stairs. "Fine, but don't tell him I was the one to lead you to him. He's going to nail my balls to the wall."

"I think Kyle would have something to say about that."

Dennis snorted. "The way he babies his siblings, I don't think he feels either of them can do any wrong. He'd probably tell me I should be more careful with my tools or something."

Drake laughed, but it didn't last long. He followed Dennis upstairs in silence, and eventually, they stopped in front of a door.

Drake stared. "This is it?"

"It is. He's probably not going to let you in."

"Like I said, I don't need to be let in." Drake raised his hand and knocked. "Chris? It's Drake. I'd like to talk to you, and I'd rather do it face-to-face, but if you're not up for that, we can do it through the door. Just give me a sign, all right?"

Drake held his breath, wondering what that sign would be. He got his answer when Chris swung the door open.

Chris's first instinct when he heard Drake outside his bed-room had been to hide in his bed. If he didn't answer, Drake would go away, and Chris wouldn't have to deal with him.

But part of him *wanted* to deal with him. His wolf yearned to spend time with their mate, maybe even to shift and go for a run with him. It had been too long since Chris had allowed himself to shift and play around, mostly because he didn't feel secure in his position here. He doubted any pride member would attack him or do anything stupid like that, but he was trying to protect himself.

Maybe he'd been going about this wrong. Maybe instead of protecting himself, he should allow himself to be happy. Was there a chance he'd get hurt? Of course there was. Even though Drake was his mate, they would still fight and yell at each other. Hell, Kyle's relationship with Dennis had started on shaky legs because of what Kyle had done, yet Dennis had still fallen in love with him. At least Chris hadn't done something stupid like try to take over the pride.

So Chris had taken a chance. He didn't know how things would end, but they hadn't even started yet, and it was because of him. He needed to be the one to take that first step. Drake had already taken half a step for him since he was here. He was so close that Chris just had to reach out, and he'd have him.

His bedroom was a mess, but Drake might as well see Chris as he really was. Hopefully, Drake wasn't a neat freak. Even when Chris felt good and actively kept his living space neat, he was a bit of a mess.

Drake beamed as if Chris was the best thing he'd ever seen. "I wasn't sure you'd open it," he said.

Chris shuffled his feet. "I wasn't sure I'd open it, either."

Drake nodded seriously, as if he understood.

Maybe he did, but Chris couldn't know since he didn't know his mate.

"I get it. It's overwhelming, isn't it? One day, you're on your own, and the next, your mate is thrown at you, and you don't know what to do with him."

"Pretty much," Chris said with a smile.

"There's also the fact that you just arrived in town. You probably don't know anyone here. Well, you have the pride, of course, but I can't imagine that you instantly became best friends with the members. I don't know about you, but it always takes me a while to warm up to people. Maybe I'd be hiding in my bedroom, too, if I were in your place."

Like last time, Drake was a mess. Words seemed to spill out of his mouth without any control on his part. Chris had found it slightly annoying when they'd met, but now, he thought it was adorable. It helped him feel more comfortable, especially since Dennis was standing there, his gaze bouncing from one to the other like a ping-pong ball.

"I wasn't sure I should show him where your room was," Dennis said slowly.

"It's fine. He's fine."

Drake wiggled his eyebrows. "I am, aren't I? Can you believe that Karl suggested I needed to lose weight?"

Maybe if Chris focused on beating Karl's ass, it would be easier for him to leave his bedroom. He wanted to ask the guy what the fuck he was thinking. Drake didn't need to lose weight. He was perfect just the way he was. "Did he?"

Drake laughed. "He did, but he was an asshole, so I'm not surprised I wasn't the right person for him. After all, I'm the right person for *you*." He seemed a bit shy as he looked down at his feet, and Chris's heart stuttered.

This was his mate, the man he was supposed to spend the rest of his life with. He'd been afraid of that, but spending a few minutes with Drake was enough to show Chris that maybe he didn't need to be.

He stepped to the side. "Why don't you come in? You're here to talk, aren't you?"

Drake's eyes went wide. "I am, but I don't have to be in your bedroom to talk to you."

"Does that mean you don't want to come in?"

"It means I don't want you to feel like you have to invite me in just because I'm here. I can stay in the hallway, or we can go downstairs or even leave the house." Drake's gaze flickered over Chris's body. "Although you might want to change if you want to go into town. I like your style, but most people don't usually wear pajamas to walk around."

Chris huffed. "I'm wondering if you should have been my sister's mate. What do you have against comfortable pajamas?"

"Nothing," Drake said. "They're just not the height of

fashion."

Chris shook his head and gestured at Drake to come in. "Good thing only you and my four walls will see me, then."

"You do realize I'm still here," Dennis said.

Chris grinned at him. "Not for long. You can run to my brother and tell him about this. I'm sure he'll be happy to know that Drake's finally here to drag me out of bed."

"Or keep you in it," Drake teased before slapping his hand over his mouth. "I'm sorry. I tend to talk a lot when I'm nervous, and you make me very nervous," he confessed.

Chris was still laughing as he closed the door in Dennis's face. He looked around the room, but it was still as much of a mess as it had been five minutes ago, so he gestured to the bed. "Why don't you sit down?"

Drake's eyes were huge as he looked from Chris to the bed. For a moment, Chris wondered if he'd said something wrong, but he was sure he hadn't propositioned him. He'd remember that.

Drake sat on the very edge of the mattress, as if he was ready to bolt. Maybe he expected Chris to kick him out once they had their chat. Chris hated that he'd pushed his mate away so hard that Drake felt that way, but this was his chance to fix that.

"How are you feeling?" Drake asked instead of getting straight to the point like Chris had expected him to.

"I'm fine. I mean, physically, there's nothing wrong with me."

"There doesn't need to be something wrong with you for you not to feel okay. You don't have to lie to me, Chris. No matter what you say, I'll be there to support you, and I won't tell anyone."

"Not even Dennis and my brother?"

"Especially not them. I know how nosy family can be."

"You have a big family?"

Drake shrugged. "Not really. I had a pack, but I'm kind of a loner, so I'd rather have only a few selected people in my life."

"And I'm one of those selected people?"

"You, Dennis, Taylor, and Jacob. Oh, and Kyle now, too, although not everyone is convinced he isn't going to kill Gal in his sleep to take over the pride."

It was said with a smile, so Chris was pretty sure Drake was teasing, but still. "People still think my brother wants the pride?"

"Not really. He's happy with Dennis, and Dennis would kick his ass if he did something like that."

"What about becoming a pride member? Would you want to do that?" Chris had doubts, considering Drake had just told him he was a loner, but Chris wasn't going anywhere. The pride was where his family lived, and he had no intention of abandoning them.

Not that moving into town would be abandoning his family, but it wasn't something Chris was willing to consider. The pride was his home now, and hopefully, it could be Drake's home soon, too.

Drake wasn't surprised by Chris's question. Chris had only recently become a pride member, as had his family. It made sense that he wouldn't want to leave anytime soon.

"I wouldn't say no if I had a good reason to become a pride member," Drake offered. "I've only heard good things about the pride and Gal since I moved into town a few years ago, but I know things aren't always like that."

Chris shrugged. "I wouldn't know. The old alpha is my brother's father, but I never knew him, and Gal was already in charge when we arrived."

"I guess I can visit more often and see if it's something I

might like. I don't think I would say no if you asked me, and Dennis and the others have been trying to convince me since I arrived in town. They really want me to be a pride member."

"I think I do, too," Chris murmured.

"Then I'll think about it. I'm not making any promises, but I'm pretty sure my answer will be yes."

"Because your mate is asking?"

"And because it's not like I hated being part of a pack. I'm pretty sure I disliked the pack members more than being part of the pack itself. When people are insufferable, it doesn't get any better just because they're part of a pack."

Chris's lips twitched as if he was repressing a smile. "Oh?"

"I have many stories if you ever want to hear them, but I think that right now, we should be talking about something more important."

Chris grimaced. "I guess we should. Where does this leave us, then? What do you expect from me and from our bond?"

"Well, for one, I don't want you to think that we have to bond."

Chris blinked as if he didn't quite understand what Drake was saying.

Drake knew why. He'd just offered not to bond with his mate, and it probably didn't make a lot of sense.

"What do you mean?" Chris asked.

"Exactly what I said. Both of us are shifters, which means we'll live long lives. We don't have to bond to a human mate to ensure they won't age faster than we do. We can take our time, even if it takes years, or you can decide you don't want to bond, and that'll be fine with me, too."

"How can it be fine? Don't you want to bond with me?"

"Of course I want to bond with you, but not if it's going to scare you and push you away. If I have to choose between being bonded to you but not having you in my life because you're too scared and not bonding with you but being happy,

I know what I'll choose."

"I don't understand you."

Drake snorted. "I think a lot of people don't understand me. It's why they tend to run away once they get to know me a bit better." Drake hesitated. He'd sworn to himself that he would do his best to change to make it easier for Chris to accept him and welcome him into his life, but maybe he should still give Chris a warning. "I can be a lot," he confessed. "My last boyfriend dumped me because he thought I talked too much."

"Do you happen to know where he lives?" Chris asked casually.

"No. Why?" The less Drake thought about the guy, the better he felt. Why would he want to know where he lived?

Chris shrugged. "I don't know. I was just curious, I guess."

"Well, be curious about me, not about my ex-boyfriend."

Chris gestured at Drake to continue, but it took Drake a second to remember what he was talking about. "Right. I'm not going to talk about my exes, but you should probably know that most of them felt like I was too much to deal with. It's why they left me."

"You still don't remember that address?"

Drake couldn't help but smile. He couldn't believe that Chris was already making him happier than he'd ever been in any of his past relationships. "I'm not letting you go there and beat him up. It doesn't matter anyway, because he's in the past, but you're in the future."

Chris's cheeks flushed. "You really think so?"

"We're mates, aren't we? Of course I think so. I don't know what the future will be like and how things will be between us, but yeah. I want that with you."

"So let me get this straight—you want whatever I'm willing to give you, and you don't care if you have to wait for weeks or even longer. You can even accept that you might never bond with me."

Drake leaned closer. "I only care about you and your happiness."

He suspected it would take some time for Chris to believe him. He looked like he hadn't had a lot of happiness in his life, and Drake hated that for him. Luckily for Chris, he was here now, and he could help him.

He'd make Chris the happiest man on earth.

"It's hard to believe that," Chris murmured.

"Well, I'm your mate, so I'm kind of supposed to be interested in your happiness. I guess I know that mates don't always work out, but the majority of them do, and they're very happy. I've met many mated couples over the years, and you know when they're happier? When they're doing something that makes their mate happy. That's what I always think about when I think about my mate and what I aim for when it comes to you." He cringed. "And I'm talking a lot again, aren't I? I'm really sorry. You need to tell me if I'm taking over conversations. You could even smack me. Usually, that's enough to get me to shut up, but I should probably not tell you how I know, because you would threaten another ex if I did."

Chris reached for Drake.

For a second, Drake expected to be hit. Carson hadn't smacked him hard, but it had still hurt, mostly Drake's heart and soul. He'd deserved it, though. He couldn't keep his mouth shut to save his life.

But Chris didn't smack Drake. Instead, he hooked a hand around the back of his neck and pulled him forward.

Drake yielded easily, allowing Chris to manhandle him until he had him where he wanted.

Apparently, that was close enough to kiss, because the next thing Drake knew, their lips were pressed together.

The kiss didn't last long. Chris let go of Drake almost as

soon as their lips touched, and while Drake lingered for a second, wanting more, he already knew he would need to do this at Chris's pace. If all Chris wanted was to press his lips together, that was fine with Drake.

It had to be.

When Chris leaned back, his cheeks were flushed. "I'm not going to smack you because you like talking," he said.

"Thank you. It wasn't great when it happened."

"Am I going to want to strangle all of your exes? Because so far, it doesn't sound like you have any good ones."

They both leaned away, but Chris slid his hand off Drake's neck and linked their fingers together instead.

That made Drake's heart race. He told himself to stop being an idiot. This wasn't his first crush. It was his mate, and he didn't want to make a fool of himself.

He suspected he already had, but still.

"I told you that I'm a lot to deal with," he explained. "Most of my exes didn't want that. They'd stay with me for a few months before fleeing. I can't even blame them for not wanting to stay with someone they couldn't stand. Besides, it's for the best, because it means I was single when I met you."

"You almost weren't," Chris muttered under his breath.

"I never would've gone home with Karl. He was obnoxious and rude, even though he was pretty."

"You're prettier."

Chris's cheeks flushed again, and Drake had to resist the urge to lean over and kiss him. Clearly, coming here had been the right decision. Chris was still holding his hand, and they'd kissed. If this was all Chris was willing to give Drake, Drake would be happy. In fact, he couldn't be happier.

Things were finally moving forward. He didn't need them to rush ahead, just to keep taking tiny steps toward their future.

CHAPTER FOUR

Chris was finally out of his bedroom. He still felt the need to run back and hide, but the house was fairly empty since it was the middle of the morning, and it helped. What also helped was knowing that later today, he would see Drake. He didn't know what they would do together, but they'd taken a massive step forward in their relationship the other day, and it felt like doing so had helped get Chris over whatever his problem had been.

It had been a lot to take in, and he'd broken down a little. Now that he'd taken time to wrap his mind around everything, his brain was finally making sense of it, and he wasn't frightened anymore.

Well, not much, anyway.

Being a pride member was still intimidating. Chris didn't know what he would do if he crossed paths with any of the pride members today. They knew who he was, and they'd welcomed his family into the pride, but he was a bit of a mystery to them, just like the pride was a mystery to him. He kind of wished he could fast forward and get to the point where he was comfortable, but that would take work, and he was the only one who could do that work.

He peeked into the kitchen, relieved to see it was empty. He scurried to the fridge, feeling like he was doing something he shouldn't be doing even though he'd been told that everyone was welcome to eat whatever food they found in the communal areas of the house as long as they wrote it down on the grocery list. He could take whatever he wanted, so after checking what was inside, he grabbed some fruit.

He closed the fridge and turned, wondering if he should go back to his room or eat outside since, even though it was cold, it was a nice day. He froze at the sight of someone standing there, watching him.

"You scared me," he said.

The man looked unapologetic. "I feel you deserve it."

"Why?"

"Because of what you've been doing to my friend."

Chris opened the containers of strawberries. They'd already been washed, so he popped one into his mouth as he tried to make sense of what the man was saying. "You're going to have to be more specific."

"Why? Do you play with the heart of many guys?"

"I don't have any idea what you're talking about. I'm not playing with anyone's heart."

"Are you sure? Because Drake's been all over the place since he's met you."

Chris finally understood. This had to be one of Drake and Dennis's friends. He knew there were four — five if he counted Dennis's human friend Eddie — and they were close. The three who belonged to the pride wanted Drake to become a pride member, and Chris wasn't sure if his presence with the pride helped that cause or complicated it. "I'm not playing with Drake," he promised. They had a date later, and he was taking it seriously.

"What are you doing, then?"

Chris had no intention of spilling everything to a stranger. He didn't even know the guy's name, even though he had a vague idea who he was. "Trying to wrap my mind around losing my mother, my home, and finding my mate. I'm sorry if to you it looks like I'm taking too much time, but I *need* that time."

The guy had the good taste of looking sorry. "Right. Dennis

mentioned that you lost your mother, but I forgot."

"Maybe you should try to remember all the information before you judge a guy you don't know."

"Only if you do the same with Drake."

Chris didn't understand. "What do you mean?"

"Drake's in love with love. He's been trying to find someone for as long as I've known him. His main goal was to find his mate, of course, but he dated, and every time, it ended the same way."

"I don't particularly want to think about my mate dating other people. It was bad enough that I met him while he was on a date with another guy."

The man flopped his hand. "Those guys don't matter. Only you do, which you'd know if you'd talked to Drake."

"I did."

The man rolled his eyes. "Clearly, not long enough. What I was trying to say is that those guys all tried to change Drake. They kept telling him he was too much, and he made himself smaller to fit with them. Don't do that to him. I know you're his mate, but if you feel you can't let him be himself, you need to let him go."

Chris set the strawberries on the counter and crossed his arms over his chest. He was feeling defensive, because even though he'd run away from Drake, it didn't mean he was an asshole or that he had the intention of molding Drake into a man he wasn't. "Like you said, those men don't matter," he pointed out. "They weren't his mate. I am, and I want to make him happy."

The man stared at him for a moment before grinning and sticking his hand out. "Jacob."

"Obviously, you already know who I am." Chris shook his hand before quickly stepping back.

"My best friend's mate. Welcome to the pride, Chris."

This felt like a kind of shovel talk but without any mention of the shovel. Chris had no doubt that Jacob would kick his ass if he ever dared make Drake think that he had to change. Chris kind of wanted to find all of Drake's ex-boyfriends and kick their asses, so he got it. From what little he'd heard about them, they'd deserve it.

"I'm, uh, going to go," he said, gesturing at the door.

He left the kitchen, ignoring the way Jacob laughed at him as he almost ran away. He wasn't sure where he was going, but he continued rushing and turning corners until he was sure Jacob wasn't following him to threaten him.

Dammit. He'd left the strawberries in the kitchen.

He looked around the hallway, relaxing when he recognized it. He might have spent a lot of time in his bedroom, but he was starting to recognize the various places in the house. He was by the library, and since he was here, he decided he might as well check it out. His grandfather loved the place. Maybe he was there, and he and Chris could spend time together.

Chris pushed open the door and walked in, only to freeze. He gaped in horror at the sight in front of him. "What are you doing?"

His grandfather jumped off the couch, but when the lady he'd been kissing tried to do the same, he shook his head at her and helped her to sit back down. "Christopher," he began.

"Nope," Chris said, shaking his head.

Chris's grandfather glared at him. "Did you have a reason to interrupt us?"

"Of course I did. I didn't want to watch you kissing someone."

"I don't see how it's any of your business."

"You're my grandfather. Anything you do is my business."

That was the wrong thing to say. Chris's grandfather put his hands on his hips and narrowed his eyes at him. "Christopher," he repeated. "I'm an adult. I don't need your benediction or your authorization to kiss someone."

Chris rubbed his face. "I know. That's not what I was saying. I just didn't expect it, all right?" Kyle had found his mate, and now their grandfather had a girlfriend. Jennifer had Annabelle, while Chris had — he had Drake.

Chris wasn't alone. It was hard to remember sometimes, but he hoped it would get easier.

"This is Agatha," his grandfather said. "She's a dear friend of mine."

Chris arched an eyebrow. "Just a friend?"

His grandfather's smile turned soft and gooey, which made Chris look away because he didn't want to see *that*.

"For now," his grandfather confirmed.

Agatha sighed, and Chris had to resist the urge to run away screaming when he saw the mopey smile she was giving William.

"Well, I'm happy for you," he told his grandpa.

"Are you sure? You don't sound or look happy."

"I was just thinking about how Kyle has his mate, and Jennifer has her friends, and I realized that I have someone, too."

William nodded. "Your mate."

"Sorry I didn't tell you."

"I'm sorry I had to learn about your mate from your brother, but it's okay. I understand that these past few weeks have been overwhelming for you, and you were trying to deal with all of it as best as you could. I was getting worried, though. I wasn't sure you'd ever come out of your bedroom."

"Well, here I am." And Chris kind of wished he could go back to his bedroom. His one foray out in the pride house had led to him being given a talking-to by Jacob and walking in on his grandfather kissing his girlfriend. What was next? Kyle and Dennis having sex?

Chris shuddered in horror. He wouldn't survive that.

"I just talked to your mate," Jacob announced.

Drake squinted at his phone. Having this video call with his friends on such a small screen wasn't the best idea, but he needed their help.

He and Chris were going on a date. Chris had initiated it, and while Drake had been nervous after the way things had started between them, he hadn't been able to say no. He hadn't wanted to say no. He wanted to go on a date with Chris and talk to him for hours. He wanted them to look at the stars and make out at the back of a movie theater. He wanted them to be together and talk as if they were the only ones in the restaurant.

He wanted to spend time with his mate.

It looked like he was getting his wish, but he wanted to make a good impression, which was where this call came into play. "Aren't we supposed to tell him how to dress?" Taylor asked.

"We can tell him while I also explain what happened with Chris," Jacob answered. "And take off that shirt. Red is *not* your color."

Drake looked down at himself. "It's one of my favorites."

"It might be your favorite, but it doesn't mean it doesn't make you look washed out."

Great. Now Drake wouldn't want to wear his favorite shirt anymore. Apparently, it washed him out.

"Don't listen to him," Dennis said. "You look good, and if you want to wear that shirt, you should go for it."

"Why am I in on this conversation again?" Eddie asked.

Drake didn't know Eddie as well as Dennis did. He didn't think Jacob and Taylor did, either. Eddie was closer to Dennis, which might be because he was human and didn't live with the pride.

Taylor, Jacob, and Dennis had grown up together. Drake

had moved to Green Hill only a few years ago, but they'd become fast friends after playing around in their shifted form for a bit. Eddie's case was more complicated. He was close to Dennis, but Drake wasn't sure he had anything in common with the guy. Still, he didn't mind having him on this call.

Even though he didn't know why he was there, either.

"We just have to find the perfect outfit," Taylor said. "How about that blue shirt you wore this summer? You know, when you came over for the barbecue?"

"I couldn't get the red wine out of it," Drake said with a grimace. "I threw it away."

"It would have made your eyes pop out," Taylor complained.

"Well, it's not an option, so let's focus on the things I do have in my closet."

Drake turned to face it. He and Chris weren't doing anything weird for the date, which was a good thing because if they were, Drake would probably be freaking out even more. It was bad enough that he had no idea what to wear. He wanted to make a good impression, even though Chris was his mate and he was supposed to want him as he was.

"The guy's your mate, right?" Eddie asked.

Drake squinted at his tiny face on his phone. "Yeah, he is."

"Then does it matter what you wear? Aren't you going to end up naked, anyway?"

Drake spluttered. "Not tonight. We just met, and we're taking things slow."

"But you already know you're going to end up together."

"It doesn't mean we have to rush into things." Especially since Chris was new in town. It was already hard enough for him to deal with everything.

"I get that, and I get wanting to look good for your mate, but I feel you're worrying a bit too much. I'm pretty sure your guy would like you even if you wore a garbage bag over your head. I mean, I understand being nervous for a first date or whatever, but again, if he's your mate, you already know you'll end up together eventually. Maybe try to relax and think about that? You don't have to impress him or anything. He's already yours."

It was true, but it didn't help. Drake believed that Fate paired up mates because they were perfect for each other, which meant he had to be perfect for Chris, but he didn't feel like he was. He'd never been perfect for anyone else. Everyone always had a problem with him — he talked too much, he was too clingy, he was too much in general. He'd been dumped several times because of that, and while he didn't think Chris was going to leave him anytime soon, he wasn't willing to risk it.

Hence the need to look good.

"He's not wrong," Dennis pointed out. "You don't know each other well, but he's yours, and you're his. You just have to relax and be yourself."

Drake had already decided he couldn't be. Being himself meant sending Chris running, and that was one thing he couldn't do. If he had to tone it down and act like a shadow of himself, he'd do it. It would probably hurt once Chris realized what was going on, but hopefully, he'd already have fallen in love with Drake by the time that happened.

"Just so you know, Chris just left the house," Dennis announced. "Kyle says he looked nice."

Drake glanced down at himself. He'd taken off the red shirt and had put on a green one. This meant no more changing for him, so he grabbed a sweater and pulled it on over the shirt. It was getting cold, and he didn't want to go through this date with chattering teeth.

"You look good," Taylor declared.

There were murmurs of assent from the others, but Drake ignored them as he tried to smooth down his hair.

"Don't worry too much," Dennis said in a gentle voice. "You might have had a rocky start, but you're not the only ones. Just think about me and Kyle. If we managed to get over the mess Kyle made, you can do this."

Drake prayed he was right. He wanted to head out after hanging up, but Chris wasn't here yet, so instead, he started pacing. It wouldn't take long for Chris to arrive. Nothing was very far in Green Hill.

When he heard the knock, he rushed to his front door. His foot caught on a shoe he'd abandoned by the door, and he fell forward, slamming against the wall.

"Drake? Everything okay?" Chris asked from outside.

Drake groaned and buried his face in his hands. Why was he like this? Why was he so clumsy and messed up? Couldn't he be smooth and suave instead? That was what he needed to be to get Chris to give him a chance, dammit.

He opened the door, doing his best not to look Chris in the eyes. "I'm fine. Just let me grab my jacket, and I'll be ready to go."

Chris nodded slowly. He was staring at Drake as if trying to check if he'd hurt himself, so Drake gave him a wide smile and turned.

Only to stumble on the shoe again.

He swore under his breath and kicked it to the side, grabbed his jacket, wallet, and everything else, and stepped out. He closed his apartment door, wrinkling his nose at the heavy scent of garlic in the air. Someone in the building was cooking.

He'd been so nervous at the thought of going on a date with Chris that he'd barely eaten today. His stomach chose that moment to remind him of that. It growled loudly enough that Chris cocked his head, and Drake wanted the floor to swallow him.

"Sorry about that," he said.

"Not a problem. If you're that hungry, we should probably move faster. You'll feel better once you eat something."

"Oh, I don't feel bad."

"You don't? Because that sounded like you're starving."

"I'm just a bit hungry."

Chris didn't look convinced, but he nodded. When a hand landed on Drake's back, he jerked forward and immediately regretted it because it caused Chris to drop his hand. Drake wanted Chris to touch him again, but he couldn't ask, so instead, he gave him a tight smile and made a beeline for the elevator.

So far, their first date wasn't going great.

"What did you do today?" Chris asked.

"Not much. I went to work, cleaned the house, and got ready for our date."

"Did you freak out like I did?"

"Oh, yeah. I'm still freaking out, actually," Drake said before he remembered he shouldn't be himself and blurt out everything he was feeling to Chris.

This date was going to be a disaster, wasn't it?

Chris could tell that Drake regretted blurting that out, but he didn't mind. They were mates, which meant they weren't playing games. They should be telling each other how they felt, and they shouldn't be ashamed of it.

"You don't have to freak out," he gently said as they stepped into the elevator. "It's just me."

Drake snorted, then visibly curled in on himself as if he expected Chris to be angry at his reaction. He was all over the place, and Chris wasn't sure what was happening, but being angry was the last thing on his mind.

"How am I not supposed to freak out? I feel that way *because* you're my mate, not in spite of it."

"Because there's so much riding on this relationship, right?" Chris offered. "We're supposed to love each other's life. We don't know that yet, though. I mean, I like you, but I can't say it's love yet. It will be, eventually. That's all that matters in the end."

Drake's eyes were wide. He stared at Chris, and Chris wished he could read his mind, because he didn't understand him. Drake had to be the most confusing person he'd ever met, and he loved it. He loved the feeling of being kept on his toes, yet at the same time, he knew that Drake would never do anything to hurt him intentionally. He wasn't quite ready to hand his heart over to Drake, but he felt it would be a possibility somewhere down the road, and he was ready for it.

Well, mostly.

The elevator dinged, and the doors slid open. Drake's attention snapped to that, and he rushed out as if he couldn't wait to get away from Chris. His foot caught on something, and he stumbled forward.

Chris managed to grab him around the waist and hauled him back in. Drake's body collided with his, momentarily knocking the breath out of him. His back hit the elevator wall, and for a second, both he and Drake fell silent and still.

"Sorry," Drake muttered.

"Not a problem, but you should watch where you put your feet."

Drake mumbled something before carefully leaving the elevator. Chris was behind him, watching him. He couldn't make sense of this. He was sure this wasn't the way Drake behaved when he was with his friends or with people he felt comfortable with. It might be because he didn't know how Chris would react to his personality and wasn't willing to risk it. Chris wanted to tell him he didn't have to worry about that, and he could.

"You know, I *really* like you," he said as he followed Drake out of the building.

Drake stumbled again, but this time, he didn't need Chris's help to stay on his feet. "You really do?"

"Yeah. I like that you always have something to say. I like that you're never silent." Because silence meant too much time to obsess over his thoughts, and that wasn't something Chris wanted to do. He'd have to deal with all of that eventually, but not right now. Not during his first date with his mate.

"You don't want me to stop talking so much?"

"Why would I want that? You being a chatterbox is part of your charm, and I *am* charmed."

Drake's cheeks flushed. "I'm charmed, too."

"Then let's go eat something and charm each other." Chris offered Drake his hand. For a second, Drake stared at it as if it might bite him.

Chris wasn't into biting, but he wouldn't be against pinching if they were closer.

Drake finally took Chris's hand, and Chris linked their fingers together. He pulled Drake toward his car.

"Dennis recommended this place," he explained as he drove them to the restaurant. "He said it's nice but not too nice, if you know what I mean."

"You mean the kind of place where I'll try hard not to laugh because everyone would stare at me if I did?"

"Yes. I don't like that kind of place, either."

Drake bounced a bit in his seat. "Once I went to a place like that with my parents, and there was this lady with red lipstick and black sunglasses. I mean, she had on the sunglasses inside, like an asshole. Anyway, she was kind of weird, but she wasn't the problem. The problem was her Chihuahua."

Chris smiled as he listened to Drake babble about the Chihuahua and how it had attacked him, which had made him turn into his aardwolf just before they were taken to their table.

"No one saw me shifting, and my father quickly bundled up my clothes and hid them under his jacket. He looked pregnant, but it was kind of a lumpy pregnant belly. Anyway, when the waitress saw him, she did a double take."

Chris grinned. The way Drake had of telling the story was so vivid that it felt like he was there. "She didn't realize that he hadn't looked pregnant before?" And that he was a guy?

"I think she probably did but didn't want to say anything about it. Besides, she got immediately distracted by me. I don't know if you looked up what kind of shifter I am, but we don't exactly look like dogs."

They didn't. In fact, aardwolves looked like tiny hyenas. "So she didn't think you were a dog."

"It was clear she didn't know what to make of me, and she kept looking between me and my father as if trying to understand what to do first. Eventually, she ignored my father and told my mother that animals weren't allowed in the restaurant."

"What about the Chihuahua?"

"Apparently, he was a service animal, and the waitress couldn't do anything about him, even though he was eating straight from a plate." Drake shuddered dramatically. "I know they wash all those dishes and everything, but can you imagine eating on that plate once the Chihuahua was done with it?"

"I don't think I would've eaten in that restaurant, to be honest."

"We didn't, either, but that's because my mother made a scene. She pointed out the Chihuahua couldn't be a service animal, and she wasn't wrong, but then I started crying, and let me tell you, when I'm in that form, it's an odd sound. The waitress freaked out and thought I was attacking her, so she ran away. My parents and I left the place without saying anything else."

"At least you didn't have to eat off the Chihuahua's plate."

Drake laughed. "I suppose that's a relief." His expression did something complicated, and from one second to the next, it was as if he shut down. His smile vanished, and his body tensed as he straightened his back. "Sorry about that."

Chris frowned. "Sorry about what?"

"You probably don't want to hear about my parents and a bad experience we had when I was a kid. We didn't even eat there."

Chris reached for Drake's hand and squeezed quickly before returning his to the steering wheel. "I want to hear your childhood stories. I want to know everything about you, including the time you were a kid and shifted in the middle of a restaurant. You don't have to hide things from me, Drake. You certainly don't have to hide yourself."

Drake shrugged. "I'm not."

But Chris could see that he very much was. It was as if every time he relaxed and allowed himself to laugh and chat, he realized what he was doing and shut it down all over again. It was disconcerting, especially because Chris really liked the man he'd gotten to know during their past conversations.

They'd started calling each other every day after Drake had visited Chris. Drake had been there for him when he tried to force himself to finally leave his bedroom, and it was in part thanks to him that they were here tonight.

Drake had helped Chris in ways he probably didn't realize, and Chris wanted to return the favor. No matter how many times he told Drake to be himself, Drake couldn't seem to bring himself to do so, at least not permanently. He was still trying to show Chris an image he didn't fit in, which meant there had to be something deeper behind that.

And Chris was going to find out what that something was. He doubted Drake would tell him, so it was a good thing that he knew Drake's friends. Hell, one of them was his brother-in-law, and Kyle and Dennis would do anything they could to help Drake.

If the end of the date went the way the start of it had, Chris would try to dig deeper. In the meantime, maybe giving Drake some space to find his footing would help.

Drake was making a mess. He'd promised himself he'd be careful during the date, but he was a disaster, and he didn't know how to stop. Every time he tried to be serious and calm, he failed. His real self ended up leaking out, and he was too scared to look at Chris and find out what he thought of it.

He was relieved when Chris finally parked, and he almost dropped to his knees to kiss the ground once he was out of the car. Instead, he sucked in a breath, squared his shoulders, and plastered a smile on his face.

Chris walked around the car to join him and frowned. "Are you all right?"

The smile almost fell, but Drake managed to keep it up. "Of course. Why wouldn't I be?"

"I don't know. You look a bit weird. If you're not feeling well, I can take you home."

Drake had tried to appear calm, and instead he'd ended up looking constipated. "I'm fine. We can get something to eat."

Chris's smile turned easy again. "Great, because I'm starving."

He took Drake's hand again, and Drake allowed himself to be guided inside the restaurant. He tried not to think about that time with his parents and the Chihuahua, but it was hard, even though the place was completely different. Why had he thought it was a good idea to tell Chris that story again?

He didn't understand how Chris could appear so relaxed. It was as if nothing Drake was doing bothered him. If he'd been any of Drake's exes, he'd never have walked into the restaurant, let alone sat down with Drake to have a meal.

"I'll be right with you with your drinks," the waitress said.

Chris smiled at her before turning to Drake. Drake opened his mouth, probably to say something stupid, but he was interrupted.

He wished he'd had the opportunity to say that stupid thing because it would have been better than what was actually happening.

"I see you moved on fast," Karl said as he stopped next to their table.

Drake blinked at him because *what*? "Moved on? From what?"

"From me." Karl looked from Drake to Chris. "I suppose I shouldn't be surprised since you dumped me for him right in front of me."

"I didn't dump you. We were never together."

"What would you call our coffee date?"

"A first date." What the fuck was happening? What was Karl doing?

"But we had a future together. I know you felt it." Karl leaned closer to Drake. "Is he forcing you to do this? Because if he is, I can help you. Just tell me, and I'll whisk you out of the restaurant and away from him. I'll keep you safe."

Drake wanted to scream and cry at the same time. Maybe even to laugh — did Karl really think he could defend Drake from Chris? Drake would pay to see that. Hell, he might get to see it without paying, given the way Chris was glaring at Karl.

"I'm not forcing him to do anything," Chris said with a remarkably calm voice.

Drake felt like he might snap, and he hadn't just been accused of abusing his mate.

"That's what you'd say, isn't it? But after what happened

at the coffee shop, I think it's clear that you are."

"He's not doing anything," Drake argued. "You're the one making a scene." People were starting to look their way, and Drake wanted nothing more than to run out of this place. He could never come back after the scene Karl was making.

"Shouldn't you go back to whoever you're here with?" Chris asked. He sounded angry now, but he was still under control.

"I'm not leaving without Drake. I won't allow you to hurt him any longer," Karl declared, looking around as if he expected the people in the restaurant to agree with him.

Drake got to his feet, wishing people would stop staring at him. "I'm going to go," he said. "I'm really sorry about this, Chris."

Chris caught Drake's hand and pulled him back down. "You're not going anywhere."

"But it's a disaster."

"I wouldn't call it a disaster, but even if it was, it's not your fault. Karl is doing everything on his own."

"Don't ignore me," Karl demanded.

But that was what Chris did. He looked around for the waitress, waving her down when he saw her. She looked like she'd rather be anywhere but here, but this was her job, so she came.

"I'm sorry, but this man is bothering us. Is there anything you can do about it?" he asked.

Her gaze bounced from Drake to Chris before stopping on Drake. "Is everyone all right?"

Drake wanted to die. She was seriously asking him if he was okay. Part of him thought it was sweet that she was ready to stand up for a man she didn't know if he was being abused, but another part of him was incredibly embarrassed.

"I'm fine," he said through gritted teeth. "If it wasn't for my disastrous blind date accusing my mate of hurting me."

The waitress paled. "Oh. I'll get the manager."

"That's probably a good idea."

"I'll protect you," Karl insisted.

Drake wanted to smack him. "Please, protect me from *you*."

Karl blinked. "What do you mean?"

"You're embarrassing me. My mate isn't abusing me. He's not hurting me, and he's not forcing me to do anything. I'm here with him because I want to be and because he's my mate."

Had there ever been a worst first date? Drake couldn't imagine so, and it could still get worse. Maybe he was about to suffocate with a piece of bread or something, and someone would have to perform a tracheotomy on him. At this point, he'd rather get that tracheotomy than continue talking to Karl.

Thankfully, the waitress returned with the manager. Since Karl was accusing Chris of being controlling, Drake took it upon himself to explain the situation. He told the man that he and Karl had gone on one date, and Karl hadn't taken it well when Drake had met his mate.

"Of course. I apologize," the manager said before turning to Karl. "I'm going to have to ask you to leave, sir."

"I'll sue you." Karl didn't seem to care much about Drake anymore. He'd finally realized that he'd gotten everyone's attention, and not in a good way.

"Feel free to do whatever you want as long as you leave," the manager said.

Drake stayed tense until Karl finally turned away. He wanted to cry. Would that help? Or would it make the date even worse?

"I'm really sorry about this," the manager said as he turned toward Drake and Chris. "I'll comp your meal."

"Could we have it as take-out?" Chris asked. "I think my mate needs to get out of here."

"Of course.."

Drake stared at his hands on top of the table. He was playing with his napkin, which was better than screaming.

"Hey," Chris said. "It wasn't your fault."

"I'm such a disaster. I can't believe Karl, of all people, decided to make a scene. I can never show my face here again."

"Then we'll get take-out. You need to relax, Drake. I don't think anyone holds you responsible for what happened. It was clear that Karl was doing everything by himself, and people heard you saying I was your mate. I guarantee you that they have a worse opinion of Karl than of you."

Drake wasn't sure how that was possible, but he didn't think telling Chris would work, so he pressed his lips together. He stayed silent until the manager returned with boxes, and once they had their food, he almost ran out of the restaurant.

The problem was that he couldn't relax even once they'd left. Chris had seen all of this. He'd been a part of it. It would make sense for him to decide he wanted nothing to do with any of this, and Drake wouldn't even blame him.

He turned to Chris, an apology on his lips, ready to face whatever Chris was about to throw at him. He didn't get a word out because Chris was smiling at him in a soft way that appeared fond rather than horrified. "How about we sit on a bench and eat while looking at the stars? It's cold, but not that cold. As long as we hurry, I think we can avoid frostbite."

Drake tilted his head up. The stars *were* beautiful.

But not as beautiful as his mate.

"Yeah," he murmured. "Let's look at the stars together."

Chapter Five

Things were getting better, which wasn't something Chris had expected. He'd thought it would be harder, but he'd only had to open up once, and now, here he was.

He had no idea how he'd gotten pulled into this group, although between Dennis and Drake, it made . The problem was that neither Dennis nor Drake were here right now, so why was Chris spending time with Taylor and Jacob?

At least they were mostly ignoring him, which was what he wanted. The less they focused on him, the better it was. He didn't dislike them, but they were firmly on Drake's side, and Chris felt they didn't like him much because of how he'd left Drake on the sidewalk the first time they'd met. It was weird because why would they want to spend time with him if they didn't like him? Chris had no answer, and he didn't understand these people.

He looked around the living room, wondering what he could use as an excuse to leave. Maybe he could mention he was planning to spend time with his sister?

"You're not going anywhere," Jacob said without looking up from his phone.

"I don't know what you're talking about," Chris answered.

Jacob glanced up and rolled his eyes. He was a gorgeous man, but that wasn't what pulled people in. More than his face, Chris liked his personality. He was sassy and mouthy, and from what little Chris had seen of him, he never hesitated to tell people what he thought of them to their faces. He was never cruel about it, but if someone needed to hear some truth, he'd be there to tell them.

Apparently, that included Chris.

"You've been ready to run since you came in and saw Taylor and me sitting here," Jacob pointed out. "I'm not sure why you stayed, since you don't seem to like us very much."

"I never said I don't like you."

"You didn't have to say it. It's in the way you behave." He arched a brow. "Or are you trying to tell me that you don't wish you could be anywhere but here?"

It was true that Chris had thought about leaving when he'd walked into the living room looking for his sister and had found Taylor and Jacob instead. They might be friends with Dennis and Drake, but Chris didn't know them well, and he always felt uncomfortable meeting new people. He realized that if he didn't spend time with new people, they would never become friends, and he wanted friends, but those two parts of his personality pulled him in different directions, and he never knew which one to follow.

He hadn't had a choice. As soon as Jacob had seen him, he'd beamed at him and pointed to one of the armchairs. The order had been clear, and Chris had been unable to resist. He kind of wished he had now, but it was too late. Jacob had cornered him.

"I struggle to make friends," Chris admitted.

"You don't say?"

Chris flipped him off. "And I don't like snarky people."

"Please. You already love me, and you know it. Besides, even if you don't, it doesn't matter because Drake loves me, which means we'll be in each other's lives forever and ever."

"Just my luck," Chris muttered.

"I'll tell Drake you don't like me," Jacob threatened.

"I'll tell him you're lying."

"Why does it feel like I'm sitting in a room with two toddlers?" Taylor wondered out loud, interrupting the bickering.

He didn't look angry, so Chris forced himself to relax. Jacob wasn't wrong when he said that they'd be in each other's lives forever. With Chris being Drake's mate, he'd see a lot of Drake's close friends, and Jacob and Taylor, along with Eddie and Dennis, were it. That meant that Chris needed to get along with all of them. He didn't have to become their best friend, but they had to tolerate each other.

He wasn't sure where he and Jacob stood. Jacob had ordered him to stay, but he kept poking fun at him. Coming from anyone else, Chris might have been offended, but something told him that this was just how Jacob took care of people. He pushed and prodded until they told him how they felt, and once he knew, he took charge and solved the problem. Chris wasn't sure what he did when the problem came from the person themselves, but he thought he was going to find out soon. Jacob wouldn't let this go.

"You love kids, so that shouldn't be a problem," Jacob told Taylor.

"Yeah, but I can make kids happy by giving them a lollipop, and I can't do the same with you."

"I wouldn't mind a lollipop," Chris offered.

Taylor grinned at him. "I'm sure Drake can give you something to suck on."

Chris spluttered. He should have expected that kind of joke, really. From what Drake had told him, he and his friends were pretty boisterous when they were together. Besides, it felt as if all of them had been placed on this earth to tease Chris. Being with Drake was going to keep him on his toes, and while initially that had made him nervous, now he realized he didn't mind. Maybe that was why Drake was his mate. Maybe he needed all of this — the friendships, the snarkiness, the teasing, and of course, the love.

Because these guys loved each other. Chris had always been close to his family, but it had been kind of a necessity because no one else in the pack would let them come close. They'd all known that the alpha was angry at Chris's mother for not choosing him and for having children with other men, and even though Chris and his siblings had nothing to do with that, they'd been proof of it. The alpha led, and the pack followed, so Chris hadn't had friends. Kyle and Jennifer were his friends, he supposed, but they were also siblings, so it wasn't quite the same. Some days it felt like they were forced to love Chris because they were related, but the same couldn't be said about Taylor and Jacob.

They didn't have to be here, teasing Chris. They didn't have to work on their friendship. They might be doing this for Drake, but Chris knew that if he allowed it, they could build a strong friendship.

And he wanted it. He was surprised, because he always thought of himself as a loner, but maybe he'd been alone by necessity rather than by choice.

Either way, there was no getting rid of Jacob, Taylor, and the others, which meant that Chris would have to learn how to live with having them in his life.

"Oh, there you are," someone said.

Chris looked up to see Liam, the alpha mate, stepping into the living room. For a moment, he thought Liam had been looking for Jacob or Taylor, but instead, the man moved to sit in front of him on the coffee table. He reached out and gently patted Chris's knee, smiling gently at him. "It's nothing bad, so you can wipe that worried expression off your face," he said. "I was just looking for you because I wanted to ask how you're settling in."

Jacob snorted loudly. "He's not settling in. Can you believe that we almost had to tie him to the armchair to get him to stay and spend time with us? We're Drake's best friends."

"I don't see any rope," Liam said with an arched brow.

"That's why we didn't tie him," Jacob pointed out. "We

didn't have rope. There's still time to find some, though."

Chris decided to view those words as a threat since they sounded so much like one. He glanced at the alpha mate, wondering what he'd have to say about one of his pride members threatening to tie someone up.

Liam was smiling and kept looking from Chris to the other two. "I feel that you're making friends," he told Chris.

"Not by choice," Chris grumbled even though, yeah, he *was* becoming friends with these two.

It felt weird, but since they were in Drake's life and weren't going anywhere, and neither was Chris, Chris had decided he might as well do this. It was better than keeping his distance and making Drake sad, and Chris was starting to realize that he'd do pretty much anything for his mate, even though they hadn't met that long ago.

He'd known Drake was it for him as soon as he'd smelled him. He'd been frightened, and he still was, but he was starting to realize that there was no need for him to be afraid.

He and Drake belonged together, and that was never going to change. Everything else could, but not their bond.

Drake needed to get a grip. So far, Chris hadn't said anything, but he still didn't realize how bad Drake could get. Drake had slipped up a few times during their date, but not so badly that Chris would have noticed. He had to be careful, because if he wasn't, Chris would realize that he was a needy dork, and he wouldn't want anything to do with him anymore.

That was how it always went. Once Drake was relaxed enough in his relationship to be himself, the guys he dated ran. When they saw just how needy he was and how much time they had to dedicate to him to make him happy, they weren't willing to put in the work. Drake couldn't blame them. He was a lot, even for himself sometimes.

But Chris wasn't just a guy. He was Drake's mate, which, in theory, meant that he would love all of him, including his neediness.

Right?

Drake didn't know for sure, and he wasn't willing to risk it. If he had to, he'd hide his true self for the rest of his life. As long as Chris was happy, Drake was sure he would be, too.

Maybe if he kept telling himself that, he'd eventually believe it.

"How was your date?" Dennis asked.

He and Kyle had both come to the coffee shop today. Eddie was there, too, although he'd been mostly silent until now while Kyle and Dennis chatted. Drake had expected Dennis to turn his attention to him eventually, and he wasn't surprised the time had come.

"It was fine," he said.

Kyle arched a brow. "Just fine? Do I need to have a talk with my brother?"

"Haven't you already taught him about the birds and the bees?" Eddie asked.

Kyle narrowed his eyes. "Why are we friends again?"

"Oh, we're not really friends. You tolerate me because of Dennis."

"Right. Well, you'd better be careful, because I might not tolerate you for much longer."

"Children," Dennis intervened, sounding serene. He was used to separating bickering idiots. Eddie was usually the quiet type and didn't bicker with anyone, but it seemed he'd found a friend in Kyle.

Could they be friends if they poked at each other the entire time? Drake didn't know, but it didn't matter. Whether they liked it or not, they were in each other's lives to stay.

"The date would have been better if Karl hadn't been there," Drake explained.

"Wait, your blind date?" Kyle asked.

"Yes. I still don't know what he was doing there beyond having a meal with someone, but I haven't looked too hard into it. I don't care."

"That's the right spirit," Kyle said as he patted Drake's shoulder. "Please tell me one of you told him to fuck off, though."

Drake laughed. "Oh, it was better than that. We got him kicked out by the manager. Well, the waitress decided to get the manager involved, and we didn't actually ask for Karl to be kicked out, but you know what I mean."

Surprisingly, Kyle seemed to, because he nodded. "I never met him, but from what Chris told me about the way you two met, I can guess that Karl isn't a good person."

"I wouldn't wish him on my worst enemy. I don't actually have enemies, but still. If I did have some, I wouldn't want them to be anywhere near Karl."

Kyle grimaced. "That bad?"

"Probably even worse than you're thinking. He started yelling in the middle of the restaurant and insisting that Chris was abusing and hurting me. It was horrifying, especially in the beginning when the waitress wasn't sure who to believe. I had to tell her that Chris is my mate and that Karl didn't take it well when he found out. That's when she got the manager." Drake hesitated, but he might as well go all in. "Chris took care of me after that. He asked for our food to be put in boxes so we could take them when we left, and we had dinner sitting on a bench watching the stars."

Dennis sighed. "That sounds romantic."

"It sounds cold," Kyle snarked. "But that's what I would have expected from my brother. I hate that you had to deal with Karl, though." He looked around as if he expected Karl to walk in. "Just point him out to me if you see him, and I'll take care of him."

Drake wouldn't have been surprised by the offer if it had

come from Dennis or Eddie, but it was coming from Kyle. He didn't really know his brother-in-law beyond the fact that Kyle and Dennis were together. The two of them were still very much in the honeymoon phase, which meant that they tended to spend all their free time in their room. Dennis didn't have a lot of that since he'd opened the bakery, but he and Kyle seemed happy, and that was all that mattered in the end.

"I appreciate the offer, but I think Chris would rather deal with Karl himself if he ever comes back. I don't think he will."

"You can't know that for sure."

"There's no need to fight. Karl's an asshole and an idiot, but he doesn't have a reason to continue bothering me. He knows Chris is my mate, and we told him to fuck off twice. I'm sure he learned his lesson." And if he didn't, Drake could take care of that himself. He wasn't harmless. Karl was human, so even if he was to become violent—and Drake didn't think he would—Drake wouldn't have problems taking him down. Hell, if things came to that, he'd shift and nip at his heels. He might not be big in his aardwolf form, but he *was* big enough to do some damage if he really wanted to.

And he had no doubt he'd want to do if he ever crossed paths with Karl again.

"So meeting your ex didn't deter Chris?" Eddie asked.

Drake smacked his arm. "Karl isn't my ex. We had one failed blind date."

"The rest of my question still stands. How are things going with Chris?"

Drake glanced at Kyle. It was weird to talk about Chris when Chris's brother was right there, but unless he asked Kyle to leave, he didn't have a choice.

Kyle raised his hands. "Whatever you say, it won't leave this table. I'll always be on my brother's side, but since I know him so well, I realize he can be a bit of an asshole and that he tends to push people away and close himself off. I can help you with that if you want."

"It's not him. He's pretty perfect."

Kyle snorted. "There's nothing perfect about Chris. Trust me, I grew up with him, so I know."

"I think that what Drake was trying to say is that he feels that Chris is perfect, but he's not," Dennis declared.

Drake could feel him staring, and he knew precisely why. Kyle might know Chris like the back of his hand, but Dennis knew Drake just as well. They'd only been friends for a few years, but they'd instantly felt comfortable with each other. They still did.

"Well, no one's perfect, but you guys are mates," Kyle said.

He was frowning as if he didn't understand what Dennis was talking about. He didn't know Drake as well as the others, so it was understandable.

"You can't make yourself into a man you're not just because you think it will make it easier for Chris to accept you," Eddie said. "What happens when the two of you bond and you slip up? Because you know you will."

"We'll be bonded, so I hope nothing."

"I don't think Chris would dump you, but don't you think he deserves to know the real you? What would you think if you realized he'd been hiding his personality from you?"

He wasn't wrong, and Drake was aware of that. That didn't make it any easier for him to let go of the thought that if he wanted Chris to stay, he needed to not be himself.

It had been hammered into him time and time again that he was weird, talked too much, was too needy, and a bunch of other stuff. Over the years, he'd tried pushing all of it down, but it had never really worked.

Drake needed it to work this time around. He couldn't afford for Chris to leave him. Chris was his mate, and he was the most important relationship Drake would ever have. Even if he had to sacrifice a bit of himself to make sure Chris stayed, he felt it would be okay.

After spending what had to be one of the weirdest afternoons of his life with a bunch of Drake's friends, Chris felt pretty good about their date. Even though Drake hadn't been there, Chris had gotten to know him better, which was all he wanted. Hopefully, he'd find out many more things about Drake during their date.

He was excited. Initially, he'd been panicking and wary because he hadn't known what to expect. In the movies and books, everything was always perfect from the beginning. What they shared was special, so of course the movies made it look like it didn't take any kind of work. What kind of fated mates fought or disagreed?

But that wasn't real life. This was, and Chris was finally getting over the feeling that he didn't have anyone.

He did. His family wasn't going anywhere, even though they were now focusing on other things and people, and he had Drake. With Drake came a bunch of friends, and there would always be the pride. They were still giving him a wide berth, but he'd realized it was his fault. They didn't know what to make of him, and they couldn't get to know him, because he wasn't letting them in. Maybe he could change that.

He grabbed everything he needed from his room after getting dressed, looked around one last time, and headed out, satisfied. He wasn't taking Drake to a restaurant this time. That had led to the ugly scene with Karl, and he didn't want to go through that again. No, he had something else planned, and he hoped Drake would like it.

He made his way through the house, whistling. Some days, he couldn't recognize himself. That was how much meeting Drake had changed him, and he kind of liked it.

He hadn't liked the person he was before very much. He'd

been wary of everyone, always certain he'd lose the people he cared about, to the point that he didn't want to start caring about anyone else. He already had his family, and they were related, so they weren't going anywhere. Why did he need anyone else?

But that kind of life was lonely, and Chris was glad he was finally making changes. It would take time for him to feel part of the pride, but he was taking steps in the right direction, and eventually he'd get there. Maybe the pride would even start feeling like home.

He walked past the open living room door and reached for the front door, but before he could open it, he heard footsteps behind him.

"Hey, Chris, can I talk to you for a second?" Dennis asked.

Chris looked around him, but he couldn't see his brother. That was weird, because even though Dennis was Kyle's mate, he and Chris weren't really that close.

That was another relationship Chris had to build.

"Of course. What's going on? Is it Kyle?"

"It's not. It's Drake."

Chris frowned. Drake and Dennis were friends, so if there was anything wrong with Drake, Dennis would know. "Has something happened?" he asked, already pulling his phone out of his jeans pocket.

"No. I mean, something has happened, but he's fine."

"That's not as helpful as you seem to think it is."

"I just wanted to tell you what he's doing. I think you should know, even though he's not going to be happy."

"Well, if he doesn't want me to know, you shouldn't tell me. I don't want to break his trust."

"I get that. I don't want it, either, but it's necessary before you find yourself in a situation you don't know what to make of."

That didn't sound good, but there was only one way for

Chris to understand what was happening, and that was allowing Dennis to talk. "Fine. I'm listening."

Dennis looked around, but they were alone in the entrance. He leaned against the stair railing, looking like he was trying to find the right words.

"I don't know if Drake has told you this, but he has several exes in town. He's always been in love with love, and he's wanted a relationship since the day I met him. He tried very hard to make things work every time, but since he was single when you met him, you can guess how that went."

Chris's memory flashed back to when he'd met Drake. He'd been on a date with Karl the asshole.

"Anyway, one thing Drake's exes had in common was that they all felt the same way about him."

"They loved him until they didn't?"

"To be fair, I don't think they actually loved him. I'm not going to speculate on that, though, because they weren't my relationships. I just wanted you to know that Drake always feels like he should be the perfect partner. With the many times he's been told he's needy and too much, he's been trying to soften himself down with you. He doesn't want you to be overwhelmed or to run screaming for the hills."

Chris frowned. "That doesn't make sense. Why wouldn't I want to be with him? He's my mate."

"We've already pointed that out to him, but I think he's going to do things his way. You can expect a lot of awkwardness and glances, but he's going to take a step back and give you space. He doesn't want to appear needy or feel like he's too much for you to handle."

"Do you happen to know his exes' addresses?" Chris asked, feeling more than ever convinced he needed to beat all of them to a pulp.

Dennis chuckled. "I don't, and I believe that's a good thing, from the murderous expression on your face. I don't think the people you have to deal with to solve this situation are the exes."

Chris crossed his arms over his chest and sighed. "It's Drake. He's so convinced that he has to change to find love that he's going to lose himself if he's not careful."

"Exactly. I was afraid he wouldn't fully understand what I was saying, so I'm glad to see that you have. Drake is so used to being told he needs to change that he's decided to do exactly that for you. He's going to change so he can be a more acceptable mate."

"That's ridiculous, but thank you for telling me. I don't want him to be different. I want him to be himself because that's who Fate chose for me."

"You should probably tell him that. I already tried to convince him that you'd love him the way he is, but it's not easy for him to believe it."

"I'll try, but I can tell him that he's perfect for me a hundred times, and it doesn't mean he'll believe me."

"You keep trying," Dennis said as he patted Chris's shoulder. "You should probably go. He told us about your date tonight, and he was excited. He's going to tone it down when he sees you, but he'll break eventually. He always does."

Chris thought that was a good thing, because he loved the way Drake was independent but also how he needed him. He loved everything he'd seen in Drake, and he couldn't wait to see more of it.

It looked like he was going to have to convince Drake to show him that part of him, and he wasn't quite sure how to do that, but he knew what he wanted, and he was stubborn. The situation called for that, and maybe tonight he would manage to see more hints of the real Drake.

Chris was no stranger to trying to hide, but he was the one person Drake wasn't supposed to hide from. He hoped he'd be able to get Drake to understand that.

And if he couldn't, he'd try again and again until Drake did understand. They were mates. They were perfect for each other because of who they were. If Drake was different, he wouldn't be perfect for Chris, which meant they wouldn't be mates.

Chris just had to get him to see that.

Drake could tell there was something on Chris's mind when he picked him up at his apartment. He was nice and kissed Drake on the cheek to say hello, but he was quiet.

Chris was always quiet, so Drake wasn't initially worried. When Chris kept glancing at him, though, he knew something had happened that involved him. He couldn't think of anything he'd done, which meant it had been one of his friends.

Dennis.

He'd been so adamant when they'd talked this afternoon that Drake *knew* he had something to do with this. It was the only thing that made sense. It might have been Eddie, but he didn't live with the pride, and he wouldn't know how to contact Chris. Dennis, on the other hand, lived in the same house, and they shared Kyle. It would have been easy for him to reach Chris.

He probably had.

Drake swallowed and rubbed his palms on his thighs. What happened? What had Dennis said? It couldn't be too bad, since Chris was here and they were still going on their date, but Drake needed to know.

He couldn't believe one of his best friends had betrayed him. He understood Dennis's point of view and even why he was pushing so hard for Drake to be himself, but it was Drake's choice. Dennis didn't have a say in it, and it wasn't his business, but he'd made it his by talking to Chris.

Drake kept expecting Chris to say something, but they both stayed silent the entire drive. It was awkward and tense, and

Drake hated it.

He didn't want their date to continue like this, so as soon as they were out of the car and had enough space that one of them could step away if he needed to, he turned to Chris. "You talked to Dennis," he said.

"It's more like Dennis talked to me, but yeah. He had something to say."

"Of course he did."

"He's looking out for you."

"Or maybe he's looking out for *you*. You're his mate's brother. That trumps best friends, doesn't it? Besides, I'm not even sure I'm his best friend. It's always been the five of us. Maybe Dennis feels closer to Jacob or Taylor, or even Eddie."

"Or maybe he's worried about you and trying to look out for you," Chris repeated. "He didn't say anything bad."

"But he did say something."

"Yeah."

At least Chris wasn't going to lie. Drake had been afraid of that, and he wasn't sure what he would've done. Pushed him until he admitted what had happened? Ignored it and put on a smile?

"I don't want you to act any differently than you normally would," Chris said. "I don't care if you feel like you're needy or goofy or a nerd. I don't care what your exes said about you. You wouldn't be my mate if the real you wasn't the right man for me."

Drake blinked and told himself not to cry. He was going to kill Dennis, dammit. He'd told Chris everything. "You weren't supposed to know all of this," he croaked.

"I know, and I don't like that Dennis went behind your back when it's clear you didn't want me to know any of it, but I'm also glad he did. You wouldn't have told me, and I might not have realized what was happening until it was too late."

"Too late?"

"If the man I'm supposed to fall in love with is the real you, how could I have fallen for the fake you? I think that eventually I would've thought that things between us couldn't work, even though we're mates."

Drake sucked in a breath. "You can't say that."

"And you can't say that I wouldn't fall in love with the real you. Why would Fate have chosen you, of all people, for me if you weren't what I need?"

Drake had never thought about it like that. He'd been focused on the way he'd ruined his previous relationships, and he hadn't considered the mate angle. If he was Chris's mate, that had to mean something, right?

He sighed. "Being myself hasn't worked great for the past few years. I was terrified that it would ruin everything again, and I wasn't ready for that to happen. I'm still not."

Chris was incredibly gentle when he took Drake's hand. He linked their fingers together, and Drake found himself stepping closer because how could he not?

Chris wrapped his free arm around Drake's waist and held him close. He was tall enough to bury his face against Drake's hair. Drake was pretty sure he heard him sniff, but he wasn't offended. It wasn't as weird for a shifter to sniff his mate as it would be for a human to sniff his boyfriend.

"I can't promise you that I'll love all of you," Chris said. "I'm sure there are things you'll hate about me, too, like maybe that I never make my bed and that I'm messy or that I'm happy to let the dirty dishes pile up in the sink. I wouldn't say I'm dirty, but I *am* messy, and that's been a problem for my sister and my grandfather. It doesn't mean they love me any less, though."

"But we're not talking about dirty dishes here."

"*What* are we talking about? I already know you talk a lot and that you're passionate. I like it, Drake. If you want to talk my ear off, I'll listen to every word you have to say. I realize

I'm a quiet person, but it doesn't mean you have to be. Can you imagine if we were both like that? We'd never talk."

Drake couldn't resist anymore. He buried his face against Chris's chest, doing what he'd noticed Chris do earlier. Chris smelled like home, and Drake prayed he'd never have to give that up.

That was why he'd been so anxious about getting Chris to fall in love with him. It was why he'd tried to change himself. No one else had wanted him before, but it was important that *Chris* want him.

"Look, I can promise that if it becomes too much, I'll talk to you," Chris said. "But no more hiding. I want to fall in love with my mate, not with a weird version of him."

Drake looked up. "You want to fall in love with me?"

"Of course. I really like you, Drake. I think all I need is a little more time with you, and I'll be there."

Drake felt the same way. He'd never really understood how mates could fall in love with each other so quickly, but now he realized it was because he'd never felt the bond before. Knowing that the person in front of you was supposed to complete you and make you happy for the rest of your life helped. Technically, there was no danger with Chris. He'd be there for Drake, whatever Drake needed, which was more than Drake could say about any of his exes.

Chris smiled sweetly, and when Drake reached up to kiss him, he met him halfway. They were out in the open in the parking lot, so the kiss didn't turn deep, but it helped Drake feel more settled. Feeling Chris's arms around him, his lips on his, grounded him.

He was sure he'd have trouble reminding himself that he could let go because it was so ingrained in him not to take up too much space, but he'd do it.

Chris stepped away, but he didn't let go of Drake's hand. "Come on. Let's go."

Drake finally looked around. He'd expected another restaurant—sans Karl this time—but there were no permanent
buildings. His eyes widened when he saw the ice rink. He'd
been in Green Hill for two years, so he knew that every holi-
day, the town set up the ice rink and a few rows of stalls that
sold anything from food to warm drinks, but he'd never gone.
He'd always meant to, but things were always busy during
this time of the year.

And now, he was here with Chris.

"Have you ever skated?" Chris asked.

Drake shook his head. "I wanted to, but it feels a bit dan-
gerous to go on my own because I have no idea what I'm doing."

"I'm not going to say it's easy, but I'll help you."

"Then I'm sure I can do it."

He couldn't do it. As soon as he was on the ice, his legs
started going in opposite directions. He clung to the boards
on the side, refusing Chris's hand because he didn't want to
take him down with him. He pushed one foot forward, then
the other, and it felt like someone had yanked a carpet from
under his feet. He tilted back, and it was only by some miracle
that he didn't hit his head on the way down.

"Everything okay?" Chris asked as his face appeared
above Drake's.

"I'm not sure. I think my dignity is broken."

Chris laughed. "That's fine. You can live with no dignity,
but it would be better if you didn't hit your head." He offered
Drake his hand, and this time, Drake took it because he had
no idea how he was supposed to get to his feet on his own.

"Ready to try again?" Chris asked with a smile that would
have gotten Drake to say yes to pretty much anything.

And if Drake ended the evening with more bruises than
he'd had when it had started, it didn't matter. He also ended
the evening with more kisses from his mate than he could

ever have hoped for, and *that* was what he chose to focus on.

CHAPTER SIX

Chris could tell that Drake was nervous as soon as he opened the front door. He wasn't surprised. After all, he'd been in Drake's position not that long ago. Drake was here to talk to Gal and Liam, the alpha and the alpha mate, about becoming a pride member. Chris had done the same when he'd arrived in town with his family, so the memories were fresh in his mind.

"They'll love you," he promised.

"You can't know that. I've lived in town for a few years now, and I never asked to become a pride member. Won't Gal wonder why? Won't he be offended that I changed my mind just because I met my mate?"

Chris grabbed Drake's hand and pulled him into the entrance. He closed the door and turned to face his mate, who was wringing his hands. Chris had been nervous when he'd met Gal, but not that nervous. Drake looked like he was about to explode.

"Look, I don't know Gal well because I've only recently met him, but he doesn't strike me as a bad person or a bad alpha," Chris said, trying to soothe Drake. "You probably know him better than I do. Do you really think he'd do something like that?"

Drake sighed, and his shoulders slumped. "He wouldn't. He's a good person."

"Yeah, he is." Because it would have been easy for Gal to refuse to welcome Chris and his family into the pride after what Kyle had done. Kyle had defied Gal's authority. He'd tried to take the pride from him. He'd been an idiot, and thankfully, Gal had seen that. He hadn't held it against Kyle or his family, and now, Kyle was the happiest he'd ever been.

Chris wasn't yet, but he was getting there. He was definitely happier than he'd been in recent years. After his mother had died, he'd felt like he couldn't ever feel that way again, and he'd been terrified, but moving had been the right choice. It had brought him a new home and his mate, and now that he was finally getting out of his head, he could see he could be happy here.

"So don't obsess over this. He's going to listen to what you have to say, and he's going to welcome you into the pride."

"Even though I didn't want to be part of it until I met you?"

"I think that more than a lot of people, he can understand being wary of packs and prides and whatever. Just tell him how your birth pack made you feel. But even if you didn't have a bad experience with them, he wouldn't care. He sees the pride as a big family, and he's always happy to welcome more people into it, but it's not an obligation."

Chris still had a hard time wrapping his mind around that. *He'd* never viewed his old pack as a family. He and his family had always been isolated because his mother had refused their alpha when they were younger. It wasn't normal to be pushed away by people who were supposed to be part of your family like the pride was. It had made Chris wary of becoming a pride member, but he was glad he hadn't resisted too much. They could be happy here.

As long as Drake managed to relax and be himself.

He checked the time on his phone. "Are you ready to meet Gal? We're running a few minutes late."

Drake paled. "He's going to hate me."

Chris grabbed his arm and pulled him along. "He's not going to hate you. No one could hate you."

"I'm pretty sure Karl hates me," Drake pointed out.

"I'm pretty sure Karl only has two brain cells, and at least one of them was absent the day you met him."

Drake laughed.

Chris felt his body relax. That was what he'd been aiming for, and he was glad it was working. The more tense Drake was, the more he tended to yap and overwhelm himself. When that happened, he obsessed over trying not to be himself and being unable to make that work. It made everything worse because it was too much for him to deal with, and he panicked.

Chris didn't want him to panic now. He doubted Gal would have anything bad to say about Drake even if he did, but he knew how important it was to Drake to make a good impression. His old pack might not have been as bad or complicated as Chris's, but it didn't mean he had many good memories or experiences.

"I don't know if I can do this," Drake said as he stopped in front of the door to Gal's office.

Chris turned to reassure him, but the door flew open before he could say anything. Liam squinted at them, and his gaze stopped on Drake. "Why don't you think you can do it?"

Drake opened his mouth, closed it, and opened it again. "I'm really sorry," he blurted out.

Liam waved his words away. "I'm serious. Why are you so nervous?"

"Because you're the alpha mate, and you're intimidating."

Drake looked like he'd rather be anywhere but here, but it was too late for him to change his mind. Liam had him, and Chris could hear Gal in the office. He had to be listening to them, which meant he'd heard everything.

Liam snorted. "Intimidating? Me?"

Chris had to press his lips together. He understood where Liam was coming from. Even though he was the alpha mate, he looked gentle, which made sense because he was a gentle man. He was on the tall side, although nowhere near as tall as his mate, but he was slight, with dark blond hair and kind brown eyes. He made people feel at ease, which helped in his position.

"I suspect that's because of your position as my mate," Gal said from inside the office. "Let them in, will you?"

Liam stepped to the side. Chris walked into the office, but Drake didn't follow. He stared at Chris with wide eyes, his mouth slightly open, a wild light in his gaze.

He was panicking. Chris didn't know how to help him, but he doubted that forcing him to come into the office would do anything good. "Breathe," he said gently.

"I called the alpha mate intimidating to his face," Drake said. "He's going to kick me out of the pride, and I'm not even a real pride member yet. I ruined everything."

"Nothing bad is going to happen," Liam said. "If anything, I'm kind of happy that I'm intimidating. That's not something that happens often." He puffed out his chest. "Heard that, Gal? I'm intimidating."

Gal had clearly had enough of waiting because he appeared behind Liam. He seemed amused as he wrapped an arm around his mate's shoulders and kissed the top of his head. He could do that because he was six feet four and towered over all of them.

"So very intimidating," Gal agreed. His attention turned to Drake. "Why don't you come into the office? I promise I won't eat you."

Chris hadn't thought that Drake's eyes could go even wider, but they did. He stared at Gal as if he was contemplating running away. He actually might be, so Chris grabbed his hand and pulled him into the office. "Stop panicking," he murmured. "Gal and Liam like you. They've already made their decision, and this is just a way for you to get to know them and for them to get to know you. Just be yourself."

"That's never worked well in the past," Drake pointed out.

Chris squeezed his hand. "I don't know about that. I think it's worked pretty well between us."

Drake finally relaxed, although not a lot. He leaned against Chris as he took in the office. "It has worked pretty well with you, but you're my mate. You kind of have to accept me."

"I don't have to do anything. I accepted you because I like you, and I'm not the only one. You have your friends, don't you? They love you the way you are, as I'm sure other people do, too. You need to get out of your head."

"Have you met me?" Drake asked, sounding amused.

"We haven't yet, but we've been looking forward to it," Gal said as he closed the door.

Drake jumped, and his smile fell.

Chris sighed. They'd been making progress, and he hoped they hadn't lost all of it. At this point, Drake was nervous enough that he might run out the door screaming, and Chris wasn't ready to run after him.

But if he had to, he would.

Drake was all over the place, and he hated it. When he'd left his apartment, he'd told himself he could do this, that he could be relaxed and suave and impress the alpha and his mate. Now that he was here, he knew that he *couldn't* do it.

It didn't seem to matter. He didn't need to impress Chris because they were mates, and the alpha and the alpha mate seemed to like him even though he was a mess. It was hard to believe, and he still wasn't entirely sure he trusted whatever was going on, but as the alpha gestured at the couch under one of the wide windows, he told himself that whatever happened, it didn't matter. As long as he and Chris were happy, he didn't have to be a pride member. It would make things awkward if he and Chris couldn't move in together when they were ready, but they'd find a way to make it work. Chris didn't have to live in the pride house. Right now, he wanted to because that was where his family was, and Drake would never ask him to choose, but they had time. Even if it took them years to move in together, that would be fine.

He sat on the edge of the couch, ready to bolt, even though he didn't think he'd have a reason to. Chris rolled his eyes and pulled him back, wrapping an arm around his shoulders to slide him closer. Drake squeaked, then berated himself for making such a sound in front of the alpha.

"I've been curious about you for a while," the alpha mate said as he sat down.

Drake glanced at the alpha, his eyes widening when he saw that the man was getting drinks ready. It wasn't his job.

"I have been, too," the alpha said as he handed his mate a glass of soda. "Chris, what can I give you?"

"A soda is fine."

The alpha nodded. "Drake?"

Drake gaped. "A glass of water will be perfect, Alpha."

The alpha winced. "Please call me by my name. I realize I'm the alpha, but I've never subscribed to calling alphas by their title. I don't believe it shows respect, just tradition."

Drake licked his lips and told himself not to mess this up. He couldn't afford to. "Gal. A glass of water will be fine, thank you."

Gal gave Drake a gentle smile and went to pour the drinks.

Drake couldn't look away. His old pack hadn't been a bad place to grow up, but there had always been a wide separation between the alpha and the people he considered to be on his level and everyone else. He hadn't been treated quite like royalty, but people had to defer to him and call him by his title. It was what Drake was used to and what he'd grown up with, and it felt odd to have a man in Gal's position ask him to use his name.

"Here you go," Gal said as he handed Drake a glass of water.

He'd put ice in it, and Drake took a sip, grateful. His throat was parched.

"We talked with Dennis, Taylor, and Jacob," Gal said as he sat down next to his mate.

Drake groaned. "You shouldn't believe anything they said."

For some reason that made the alpha laugh. "That's pretty much what I expected. They only had good things to say about you, though. It's clear they love you and that you're a dear friend to them."

Drake was glad to hear that. He always questioned his relationships, especially considering why his exes had dumped him. He never wanted to be too much, be it in romantic relationships or in friendships. Over the years, his friends had met the real him, and they loved him the way he was, but it was always a gamble with new people, especially new people who mattered so much. Gal could make or break Drake's future in Green Hill. If he decided he didn't want Drake around, Drake would be forced to leave.

"They're dear friends to me, too," he admitted. "They welcomed me when I didn't know anyone here, and I don't know what I'd do without them."

"They mentioned that they told you that you could become a pride member in the past, but you refused."

Drake stared down at his glass of water. He felt Chris's arm squeeze around him, and he leaned against his side, needing the support. From everything he knew about Gal and the impression he had of him today, he didn't think Gal would hold anything against him, but he couldn't be a hundred percent sure.

He couldn't be a hundred percent sure of anything in life, though. Chris could decide to dump him tomorrow. Hell, one of them could end up under a bus at any time. No matter how scared Drake was, he felt he owed it to himself and to Chris to take a leap of trust.

"I wasn't sure it was what I wanted," he admitted. "I left my birth pack before moving to Green Hill. I can't say that things were bad there, but they weren't good, either. The way the pack is led means that everyone bows down to the alpha. He can decide what we do for a living, and he can even influence who we marry. He can't do anything about mates, of course, but any other relationship? He tries to shape them."

Gal grimaced. "That doesn't sound fun."

"It's not. My parents were mates. My mother died when I was born, and my father was forced to remarry. Well, it's more that he was strongly pushed into the marriage, but I doubt good things would have happened if he'd refused. He wouldn't have been killed or anything like that, but it would've had consequences, especially because the alpha chose one of his cousins as my father's wife. My father and his new wife had more children, which was what the alpha wanted. Anyway, what I'm trying to say is that even though the alpha wasn't abusive or violent, he still used and manipulated us. We went along with what he ordered because we were afraid that if we didn't, he'd kick us out." Drake snorted. "Which I guess he kind of did."

"I thought you'd left your pack," Chris said.

Drake put down his glass of water on the coffee table and linked his fingers together. "It's more that I left before I could get kicked out. The alpha talked to my father. He wanted me to marry one of the women in his family, I think a niece or something. I never really looked into it because I didn't care. I wasn't about to marry a woman I barely knew. I wouldn't have even if I wasn't gay, but telling the alpha all of that didn't work. It was my duty to marry the woman my alpha chose for me. I decided to leave before I could be forced into it. I don't know what he would have done if I just said no to his face, but I wasn't about to stick around and find out."

"So you had bad experiences with packs," Gal said.

"I don't know if I'd call it bad, but it certainly wasn't a walk in the park. I left, and I told myself that I didn't need a pack to survive." Drake smiled. "I was right. I *didn't* need a pack, and I've been thriving without one."

"So that's why you never wanted to become a pride member before, no matter how many times Dennis and the others asked you," Liam said.

"I didn't want to risk it, even though from everything I'd heard, you two are good leaders. I just felt it wasn't worth it, especially since it wasn't a requirement for staying in town. You even allowed me inside the house to visit my friends."

"As I said, we're a family," Gal said. "We want the pride members to feel at home here because it *is* their home. That means inviting people over and having friends outside the pride."

"I don't know how much you know about the pride before Gal became alpha," Liam interjected. "But the old alpha was an asshole. We were forbidden from leaving the house. It became worse over the years until eventually even those who had jobs outside the pride were forbidden from leaving the property. They lost everything, and for a while, I was convinced that the pride would disappear. With no money, it would have been impossible for us to continue surviving. Luckily, Gal stepped in." He shook his head. "All of this is to tell you that I understand. Overbearing alphas are never a good thing, so it makes sense that you were wary of us and the pride."

Drake could hardly believe it. It sounded like Liam truly understood where he was coming from, which seemed too good to be true. He half expected Liam and Gal to start laughing and tell him they were kidding, but it never happened.

"Well, no one is forced to do anything in our pride," Gal said. "Of course, we require that you have a job and that you contribute if you live in the house, but that's about it. The happiness of our pride members is what matters the most." He paused. "Do you think you could be happy here?" he asked Drake.

That was the million-dollar question, wasn't it? Could Drake be happy with the pride?

Chris hoped he could. He didn't want to leave his family, but he would if that was what Drake wanted and needed. Chris would never force him to stay in a place where he didn't feel at ease, but he didn't want to lose the pride like he'd lost the pack.

He'd already lost too much, from his mother to the place he'd called home for his entire life, and he wasn't sure he'd survive anything else.

Drake was still cuddled against Chris's side, and it felt like he was trying to burrow even deeper. The only way to do that would be for Drake to climb into Chris's lap, but Chris doubted he'd do it. He knew Drake wanted to make a good impression on Gal and Liam. He'd been panicking at the thought of them thinking badly of him, but everything had gone well. It was clear that, as far as Gal and Liam were concerned, Drake was already a pride member.

The decision was in Drake's hands.

"I think I could be," Drake said eventually. "It's weird and exciting and a bit scary, but yeah. Maybe it's time for me to stop being afraid of what being a pride member will mean."

"If it helps, I won't ever order you to marry anyone," Gal offered. "I wouldn't do that even if I didn't know you've met your mate. People should be free to choose who they want to be with and who to love. I also don't force pride members to become parents if that's not what they want. I don't care if the pride vanishes in ten or twenty years. Some shifter groups do, and it's the most natural thing in the world. People move, fall in love with people who belong to other prides, and that's that."

Chris looked down at Drake. They hadn't mentioned kids, and he didn't think they were ready to talk about it, let alone have them. They weren't ready for a lot of things, but that was okay. They would be eventually.

"So are you our newest pride member?" Gal asked with a smile.

The answering smile Drake gave him took Chris's breath away. He'd always found Drake attractive, but over the past few weeks, Drake had relaxed and looked more comfortable in his own skin, which made him even more beautiful. Now that he'd talked to Gal, he was behaving more naturally, which was all Chris wanted. He needed Drake to be comfortable here and to feel like this place could become his home.

Drake straightened, which unfortunately pushed him slightly away from Chris. "I believe I am," he confirmed. "If that's all right with you, I'll be staying at my apartment for a bit longer."

"We have pride members who live in town, so that's not a problem. You'll learn soon that, as a pride, we're pretty open and free. As long as they warn me, I don't have anything against pride members living in town or even a bit further away. I don't care who they marry or bond with. I don't care what job they do, but I'm always ready to help them. If you ever need anything, you just have to say the word, and Liam and I will do whatever we can to help you."

"Thank you," Drake breathed out. "It's hard to believe that I can really have this and that it's real, so thank you."

"You probably shouldn't thank us just yet," Liam warned. "You haven't met the rest of the pride. You might change your mind and run away screaming."

"I doubt I will."

Chris didn't think Drake would, either. Chris had heard about some pride members not being nice people, but that wouldn't stop Drake from being happy here. Most pride members were welcoming and warm, if a bit wary, but that would change. Eventually, both Chris and Drake would feel like they belonged, and when they did, they'd be part of the family.

Chris hadn't been left behind the way he'd feared he was. When Kyle had met Dennis and Jennifer had become such good friends with Annabelle, he'd felt like his family was abandoning him. It hadn't gotten easier after he'd found out that his grandfather was dating a tiger shifter.

But he *hadn't* been abandoned. They'd always be in his life, but they also needed to dedicate time to being happy. Chris could do the same now. It wouldn't be easy, and he and Drake would have to work hard to find their footing and make their relationship work, but that was fine with Chris. It would give him something to focus on, and the reward would be a happy future, so what more could he want?

Gal leaned forward and placed a gentle hand on one of Drake's hands. "Welcome to the pride, Drake."

Drake's smile was blinding. It made Chris want to bundle him up and drag him to his room, but instead, he let go of his mate so Drake could lean forward and pull Gal into a hug. Gal made a squeaking sound and laughed, hugging Drake back.

"Sorry about that," Drake quickly said as he moved away.

"It's fine. You don't have to be afraid of me or of what will happen if you do something without asking me first. Remember that this is a family more than a pride."

"I'll try," he promised.

Chris made a mental note to remind him every day that he

was part of this family and that Gal wanted him there. Considering what he knew of Drake, he had no doubt that it would take him time to settle and actually believe that the pride was his home. It would be Chris's job to remind him of that in the meantime, and he was ready to do it. He only ever wanted his mate to be happy, and Drake would be happy if he felt welcome within the pride.

They didn't stay long in Gal's office after that. It was clear that Drake was overwhelmed and a bit weepy, and after smiling gently at him, Liam all but kicked them out. He winked at Chris, hugged Drake, and stepped back. "I'm sure Chris wants to show you his room."

Drake's cheeks flushed, but Chris just rolled his eyes. He might not have been a pride member for long, but he already knew Liam well enough. "Very funny."

"I wasn't trying to be funny. Your mate will want to see the place where he'll spend the nights when he's here."

"Maybe I'll move into his apartment," Chris grumbled.

"If you do, let us know. We can give your room to someone else."

They probably wouldn't, but there was no way Chris would leave the house anytime soon. He might eventually, but for now, he was home.

"They're not what I expected," Drake said as they walked away.

Chris *was* going to take him to his room. He just hadn't wanted to give Liam the satisfaction. "They're pretty laid-back," Chris agreed. "My old alpha doesn't sound anything like your old alpha, but he was a dick anyway. Gal is nothing like him, and I'm glad."

"I still feel like they might regret letting me into the pride. I mean, I was on my best behavior, but I still messed up."

"They're not going to regret letting you into the pride. They wouldn't have done it if they weren't convinced it was the right thing to do. You have to give people a chance to love you for who you are instead of the version you show people. The people who actually care about you will take you as you are."

That included Chris. He didn't want another mate. He didn't want another version of his mate. He wanted Drake, with his babbling and neediness and energy. He was the perfect man for Chris.

Chris could only hope to be the perfect man for him.

Drake hoped Chris was right. It was one thing to believe your mate could like you for who you were—and he still wasn't completely convinced of that—but it was another thing entirely when it came to a bunch of people Drake barely knew. In a way, Chris *had* to like him because of the bond they shared. That didn't go for Gal or the pride, and they didn't have a reason to keep Drake happy. That meant that if they didn't like him, they wouldn't hesitate to tell him.

It hurt to think they might. Drake had been trying hard to stay away from the pride, telling himself that he didn't need them and was fine on his own, that he hadn't realized that maybe that wasn't the case. He didn't want to go back to his birth pack and had never really felt at home there, but something told him that here, he could. Maybe it was because Chris was a pride member, or maybe it was because of his friends, but Drake could see himself settling down with the pride.

But what if they didn't like him? What if they decided they didn't want him here? No matter what Gal said, he wouldn't be able to ignore it if some pride members decided that was what they wanted. He'd have to give in to their demands, even if it meant kicking Drake out.

Chris stopped walking, and since he was holding Drake's hand, Drake had to do the same. He didn't argue when Chris pulled him closer. He was curious to see what would happen, but more than that, he was always okay with Chris cuddling him.

But Chris didn't cuddle him. Instead, he looked down at him, his eyes narrow as if he were trying to read him.

"You don't believe me."

Drake looked away. It was harder to lie to Chris when he was looking him in the eyes. "I never said that."

"You don't have to say it. I can see you don't believe that the pride wants you."

"I believe that Gal wants me to be a pride member. I believe you want that, too, and Dennis and my other friends, but what about everyone else? Shouldn't they have a say in it?"

"Not really. Gal is the only one who has a say in who becomes a pride member, and he told you that you were one. Isn't that enough?"

It should be, but not for Drake. "What if they, like, revolt because they want me out? Gal will have to listen to them then."

Chris snorted and slapped his free hand over his mouth. His eyes were wide now, and Drake couldn't avoid noticing how hard he was trying not to laugh. Eventually, he broke down and did, mirth shaking his body.

Drake wasn't offended, but he was confused. He didn't understand what was so funny about this.

"Sorry, but I keep imagining some of the pride members storming Gal's office and demanding for you to be kicked out, and it's funny."

"I don't find it funny," Drake grumbled.

"That's because you think it could happen, but it won't." Chris grabbed both of Drake's shoulders. "Look, what's the worst that can happen? And don't say that someone might hold Gal at gunpoint and force him to kick you out because that's not gonna happen. Try to stay realistic."

"Everyone but you and my best friends will hate me."

"That's not realistic. Yes, some people might dislike you. Hell, some might hate you. I'm sure some pride members hate me and my family and want us out, but that doesn't mean we'll leave. Gal would never allow anyone to force his hand one way or another. Besides, why would people hate you?"

"I'm sure a lot of people hate me." It certainly felt like it most days.

"Most people don't even think about you, Drake. I know that what you've been through with your exes hasn't been great, but the fact that they were idiots and couldn't see what was in front of them isn't your problem. I'll tell you that I like you as you are as many times as you need to hear it, but you're going to have to believe it eventually."

"What if I never do?" Drake whispered.

"Then I'll keep repeating it until you do. I don't care if half the pride hates you. I don't, and I want you in my life. We can learn to navigate the pride together, all right?"

There was no way Drake could say no to that. Not being a part of the pride had been fine when he was on his own. Now that he had Chris, though, he couldn't imagine being on the outside looking in. Chris was a pride member, and it made sense that Drake was one, too.

"And don't go trying to change yourself for these people," Chris continued. "I understand that you want them to have a good impression and to like you, but that's not going to work if you show them someone who isn't you. If they're going to like you, they should like the real you, just like I do."

Drake pressed closer and kissed Chris. The middle of the hallway probably wasn't the best place to do that, but he didn't care. He wanted Chris to know how important this was to him, and he couldn't find the words, so hopefully, a kiss would work just as well.

Chris made a pleased sound deep in his throat and

wrapped his arms around Drake. He turned, making Drake squeak when his back hit the wall.

"Get a room," someone yelled from the other side of the hallway.

Drake's entire body flushed, and he tried to push Chris away, but Chris didn't let go. He flipped off whoever had spoken, then dragged Drake down the hallway, not once letting go of him. It was as if he needed Drake as close as possible, which wasn't a hardship because Drake wanted the same.

He could hardly believe he would have this for the rest of his life, but he wouldn't have it any other way. No matter how complicated things were or felt, no matter how little he believed in himself, Chris would always be there. He believed in Drake much more than Drake ever had, and maybe that was what Drake needed. Maybe eventually, he'd be able to believe in himself the way Chris did.

In the meantime, Chris would do it for him.

Drake had visited the pride house a few times, but he was so focused on the feeling of Chris walking beside him that he barely paid attention to where they were in the house. He wasn't surprised when Chris unlocked a door, though.

He pulled Drake inside, slammed the door shut, and pressed Drake against it. He was clearly intent on finishing what they'd started in the hallway, and Drake was all for it. He wanted to climb his mate like a tree, and now that they were alone, he could.

Drake pressed a kiss against Chris's jaw, then his cheek, and finally, his lips. Drake grinned at him, wide and happy, and bent to kiss Drake's neck. "What would you think about moving here?"

It took Drake's brain a second to make sense of the words. "Here as in the pride house, or here as in this bedroom which is clearly yours?"

"Technically, both. If you move into my room, you'll be

moving into the pride house."

"As happy as I am to be a pride member, I don't really care about the pride house beyond the fact that you live here."

Chris closed his teeth around the sensitive skin of Drake's neck. Drake yelped and clung harder to him. "Don't be a smartass," Chris said before licking the spot he'd just bitten.

It wasn't a mating bite, which was a relief. Drake wanted to bond with Chris—in fact, there was little he wanted more—but not right now. He felt that he needed to believe in their relationship and in himself more before they could take that step. That was all right, though. They were together, and Chris had asked him to move in with him. A mating bite on their necks wasn't going to change how they felt about each other.

Drake wouldn't call it love yet, but it would be soon. He couldn't wait, but at the same time, he wanted to explore this first phase of their relationship. He wanted to find out more about Chris, to know what Chris looked like first thing in the morning, what he liked and disliked, and how to make him smile.

"Maybe in a few weeks?" he offered.

He half expected Chris not to be happy about it, but Chris smiled again, and Drake thought everything would be okay. Chris wouldn't always like him. Sometimes, he would be annoyed at him, maybe even angry, but that was all right. They'd find a way to make things work.

Drake was sure of it.

"We can talk about it again in a few weeks," Chris promised. "And if you're not ready then, we'll talk about it a few more weeks after that. I don't want us to rush into anything, Drake. We don't have to. We have plenty of time to get to know each other and fall in love."

They wouldn't need plenty of time, because when Chris said things like that, Drake fell in love with him just a bit more. All these occasions would add up until the day Drake realized that he was head over heels in love with him and couldn't imagine his life without him.

To be fair, he already couldn't, but that was a big thing to say after they'd just agreed to take things slow.

He hoped Chris would understand his answer when he kissed him. He was at a loss for words, but he didn't think it mattered because they understood each other. When Chris reached down and grabbed Drake's ass, he didn't have to say anything for Drake to hop up and wrap his legs around his waist.

Drake enjoyed the feeling of his mate pinning him against the door. He wanted to be as close as humanly possible to his mate while still being dressed.

Chris used the fact that his body was keeping Drake upright to allow his hands to roam over his body. They were still clothed, but they didn't have to be naked for Drake to feel how hard Chris was for him. Knowing that his mate was reacting to him gave him a thrill, and he squeezed his legs around Chris's waist, enjoying the startled sound Chris made. It was quickly followed by a growl, and Chris kissed Drake harder, dominating his mouth as if he wanted to leave his imprint inside of it.

Chris slipped a hand under Drake's sweater, his fingers finding one of his nipples almost instantly. Drake moaned and threw his head back, but that didn't stop Chris from kissing him. He just moved his lips downward, trailing over Drake's neck, biting once against the spot where Drake was convinced his mating bite would be soon.

They rutted against each other, using the door to keep them from falling on their faces. It took Drake's breath away, and not just because he was pinned against the door. Anything Chris did made Drake feel like he couldn't quite breathe.

He almost *stopped* breathing when Chris pushed a hand between Drake's back and the door. It was a tight fit, but he managed to wiggle his hand into the back of Drake's jeans, cupping his ass. One of his fingers strayed too close to Drake's crack, and Drake jerked forward instinctively pushing their cocks together. The friction was maddening, and when Chris bit him again, Drake couldn't stop himself from coming.

It was fast and messy, but that was him, wasn't it? If Chris truly wanted him for who he was, then he wouldn't mind this, either.

Chris didn't stop moving. He kneaded Drake's ass and continued thrusting against him, panting against his neck as he chased his pleasure. There wasn't much Drake could do, considering the position he was in, but maybe he didn't need to do anything. Maybe this would be enough.

It had been for him.

When Chris stiffened, Drake held on harder. He cradled Chris against his body, enjoying the last shallow thrusts of his hips and Chris's warm breath on his skin. He enjoyed the sticky feeling in his underwear less, but he didn't care.

"I'm not sure this is taking things slow," Chris muttered, but he didn't move away to let Drake down.

Drake carded his fingers through his hair. "I don't know about that. We didn't even get naked."

Chris looked up, his eyes glinting with mischief. "Maybe that could be arranged."

Drake grinned. He had a list of things he wanted to do with Chris, and they had a future together during which they could do all those things.

Chris liked Drake just the way he was and wanted to be with him. It wasn't something Drake had ever truly believed he'd get, but he had it, and he wasn't letting go.

CHAPTER SEVEN

Chris looked around the table. Drake was to his right, next to Jennifer. Chris was slightly worried because those two together could probably destroy the world, but he wasn't about to stick his nose into their conversation.

On his right was his brother. Dennis was sitting on Kyle's other side, and like Jennifer and Drake, the two of them were talking. They also kept kissing, which Chris would make sure to tease them for. They would tease back because he was always kissing Drake, but he didn't care.

Who wouldn't kiss his mate if they were in his place?

His grandfather sat in front of him, and Agatha was next to him. Annabelle was there, too, because where Jennifer was, she generally was, too. Jacob, Taylor, and Eddie were present, too, since they were Drake's family.

And all of them together were Chris's.

It was still strange to see that Chris's life included so many people now. Before, he'd only had a handful of them—his grandfather and his siblings, and when she'd been alive, his mother. He'd never felt like he was part of something bigger the way he did now, and it was a complicated feeling to deal with.

"Everything all right?" Drake asked, leaning against Chris's side.

Chris's first instinct was to wrap an arm around him, so he did. He leaned down to kiss Drake, who tasted of tomato sauce and garlic since he'd chosen the lasagna. It wasn't unpleasant, so Chris kissed him again.

When he leaned back, Drake's cheeks were flushed. It always made Chris smile when he managed to get that reaction out of his mate.

"I'm fine," he promised. "More than fine, actually." He glanced around the table again. Dennis had chosen the restaurant, and the food was as good as he'd promised it would be.

"I feel the same way," Drake murmured. "It's incredible, isn't it?"

"It is, but I wouldn't have it any other way."

"I wouldn't, either. I like my life, and I'm pretty sure it's the first time I've felt that way. It's been a while, and I'm a bit bewildered."

"Well, I like my life, too, so don't worry too much. We can be bewildered together."

That earned Chris a wide smile that he wanted to kiss. Since he could, he leaned down again, but someone slapped his forearm.

He looked around Drake and glared at his sister, who stuck her tongue out at him.

"Very mature," he teased.

"At least I'm not making out with my mate at the dinner table. Is it really necessary? Because I don't want to watch my brother slobber all over his mate while I'm trying to eat."

"Leave them alone," Annabelle said. "They're cute."

Jennifer made a retching sound. Chris wasn't offended, because he knew how happy she was for him and Drake. She was teasing him the way she always had. He was glad that nothing had changed, at least not between him and his family. Everything else was different, but their love would always be the backbone of their family, and Chris wouldn't have it any other way.

"Have you two talked about bonding yet?" Chris's grandfather asked.

Drake squeaked and pushed away from Chris. "Not yet, William. It's way too soon."

Chris's grandfather waved his fork in the direction of Kyle and Dennis. "What about these two? Do you know if they're planning anything?"

Kyle groaned. "Do we really have to talk about that? Dennis and I agreed that it's too soon, and we're fine with that. Our family is still settling down in Green Hill, and I want to get to know Dennis and date him." His gaze strayed to Agatha. "Not all of us rush into marriage."

Because that was a thing now. William had asked Agatha to marry him, and she'd said yes. Chris had wanted to ask his grandfather if he was sure, since they hadn't known each other long, but he hadn't dared. Besides, he could guess his grandfather's answer.

He'd been bonded to his mate, Chris's grandmother, for decades. She'd died, and he'd been left behind to raise three children with his daughter. He'd put everything he had into it, but he didn't have to worry about them anymore. Often, he spoke as if he already had one foot in the grave, which was ridiculous, but Chris understood wanting to make the most of the time he had left. If he wished to marry Agatha, Chris wasn't going to argue. His grandfather knew what he was doing, and it was clear the two of them cared about each other.

"We're not rushing," William grumbled.

"Maybe not, but we haven't said anything about it, so you don't have a say in our relationships."

"I'm just worried about my grandsons. Is that so bad?"

Agatha leaned closer to him, and Chris looked away. He was happy that his grandfather had found love, but that didn't mean he wanted to see them making out at the dinner table.

Shit. Maybe he and Jennifer were more similar than he'd thought.

"We haven't talked about bonding," Drake said. "I haven't even moved into the pride house yet."

"Maybe you should start with that, then," Chris's grandfather said as he stared at Chris. "If the problem is that my grandson hasn't asked, he should."

"Was he so nosy even before we moved to Green Hill?" Chris asked Kyle.

"I think he was too busy being worried about everything else. Now that he doesn't have anything to do anymore, he's focused on us."

"We need to do something. Do you think that Gal could start a war with a nearby pack just so our grandfather can stop bothering us?"

"Very funny," William said, but he was smiling, so Chris wasn't too worried.

"Oh, Jennifer, you could do something. Have you met your mate? Are you hiding them?"

Jennifer rolled her eyes and threw a piece of bread at Chris's head.

"Children," Chris's grandfather scolded.

"I agree with William," Jacob declared, narrowing his eyes at Chris. "I think Drake should move in with Chris."

Chris wouldn't say he and Jacob were close, but he knew that Jacob was keeping an eye on him. For some reason, he was convinced that Chris would hurt Drake, which couldn't be further from the truth. Drake was happy, and Chris intended to keep him that way. He had no intention of running away or dumping him. They weren't ready to bond yet, but they would be eventually, and neither of them had a problem waiting. They were enjoying their relationship as it was, taking steps forward as slowly as they wished.

"Leave them alone," Dennis said.

"You know I'm fine with things the way they are, right?" Drake whispered as he leaned closer to Chris.

Chris kissed his forehead. "I know."

"You shouldn't listen to my friends. Jacob especially has been bothering me, but I know it's because he loves me."

And that was important to Drake. For a long time, he hadn't thought anyone could love him because of the way he was. The people who should have had broken up with him because he was too much, but Chris wondered if that really was what had happened. He didn't know Drake's exes, and it was a good thing because if he did, he'd knock them to the ground, but he suspected they'd been afraid.

Drake *was* a lot. There was no denying that. He worried when Chris didn't answer his texts, clung to him any opportunity he had, and when they were together, he was always in arm's reach. It was as if he was afraid that Chris would vanish if he couldn't see him, and Chris understood that for some people, that could be a lot.

Not for him. He'd yearned for this kind of love when he'd been alone. He was fine reassuring Drake any time he needed to be reassured. He'd already promised that he wasn't going anywhere, and he was planning to keep that promise. If initially Drake needed to see him at all times, Chris would be happy to humor him.

He could never be too much for Chris because he was perfect for him, and Chris had every intention of showing him until he finally believed him.

ABOUT THE AUTHOR

Catherine is the creator of several series, most of them para-normal, including the Whitedell Pride Series and the Gillham Pack Series. While she graduated in translation, she decided to go the writer's way because it was more fun to create her own stories and characters.

She's been living in Italy for more than twenty years, but she's a daughter of the North—Belgium to be precise—and she misses it so much that she's already planning to move back.

She loves pizza—probably too much—her son, her pets, and of course, books. She sneaks some reading time into her schedule every time she has five minutes free from writing, demands from her various pets and son, and lastly, house-work.

Connect with her:

lievens.catherine@gmail.com
BookBub: https://www.bookbub.com/authors/catherine-lievens
Website: https://authorcatherinelievens.com/
Facebook: https://www.facebook.com/catherine.lievens.9
Facebook Group:
https://www.facebook.com/groups/411788002341528/
Twitter: https://twitter.com/authorCLievens
Newsletter: http://eepurl.com/c-uvKn

www.ingramcontent.com/pod-product-compliance
Lightning Source LLC
Chambersburg PA
CBHW060639130626
46555CB00002B/871